YOU CAN'T RUN AWAY
FROM LOVE . . .

"Geoff——" Jenny's eyes actually pleaded. "If you see John, don't tell him where I am. *Please.*"

"Not tell him? He's come near a thousand miles to catch up with you. You're his girlfriend."

"Geoff, I can't say *why*. It's personal. Only please . . . please don't tell him."

Geoff didn't understand. How could he? Not even Jenny herself understood her feelings. All she knew was that she'd run away from a man she didn't love—and was now head-over-heels infatuated with a man she couldn't have. . . .

*NOBODY READS JUST **ONE** LUCY WALKER!*

1 The Other Girl

2 Heaven Is Here

3 The Distant Hills

4 Sweet and Faraway

5 The Call of the Pines

6 Come Home, Dear

7 Love in a Cloud

8 Follow Your Star

9 Home at Sundown

#10 Reaching for the Stars

#11 A Man Called Masters

#12 The Stranger from the North

#13 The River Is Down

#14 The One Who Kisses

#15 The Man from Outback

#16 Down in the Forest

#17 The Moonshiner

#18 Wife to Order

#19 The Ranger in the Hills

#20 Shining River

#21 Six for Heaven

#22 The Gone-away Man

#23 Kingdom of the Heart

#24 The Loving Heart

#25 Master of Ransome

#26 Joyday for Jodi

#27 The Bell Branch

#28 The Mountain That Went To The Sea

#29 Ribbons In Her Hair

#30 Monday In Summer

#31 Pepper Tree Bay

#32 Girl Alone

Available from Ballantine Books

Runaway
Girl

by
Lucy Walker

BALLANTINE BOOKS • NEW YORK

First published 1975 by Wm. Collins Sons & Co., Ltd.

© Lucy Walker 1975

SBN 345-24617-9-125

First Printing: October, 1975

Printed in the United States of America

BALLANTINE BOOKS
A Division of Random House, Inc.
201 East 50th Street, New York, N.Y. 10022

Runaway
Girl

1

Jenny leaned forward in the Land Rover, wrapped her arms round her knees, and took a deep breath.

"I can hardly believe it!" she said. "I'm actually here!"

Geoff Hallam, in the driver's seat, glanced at her, his grin as cheerful as it was friendly.

"You're here all right," he said. "You all that keen to get away, Jen?"

"Yes."

"I kind of thought that kiss you and John-o exchanged was not very hearty. What goes?"

Jenny straightened her back and tilted her chin.

"Please don't call him John-o," she said quietly. "His name is plain John. And we are not lovers."

Geoff looked straight ahead, the expression on his face deadpan. His grey eyes were slitted against the early morning light and the breeze stirred his light brown hair. His long legs moved restlessly as if some small stab of pain had touched him unexpectedly.

"So you and 'plain John' are not lovers. Since when? But don't tell me if you don't want, pal."

"Since never," Jenny said. But her smile died away sadly.

Just because John came to the homestead often, everyone in Yaraandoo assumed he had some ulterior reason, she thought. They almost wished me on him. Or him on me.

"All the same," she said aloud, "he shouldn't have sold Redcoat without my knowing."

"So you loved that big red horse better than your

life? Was that it? I've seen you galloping that nag through the bush myself, honey. You could have been heading for a fall."

"How wrong could you be?" Jenny said, exasperated. "Yes, I loved Redcoat, and he loved *me*. He would never, *never* have run me into danger?"

"I guess your father didn't think that way, or he wouldn't have given John the nod to sell that horse."

"My father was giving John the 'nod' for other reasons," Jenny began, and then broke off. She couldn't tell Geoff the whole story. *Noblesse oblige*. A girl must never tell, just as a man was honour-bound not to tell.

John Downing was the manager of the Pastoral Agency in Yaraandoo and her father had thought he would be a good match for Jenny. She could see it all now. Would things have been any different if she had known that in the first place?

She was one of three girls, and there was no son to carry on the farm in the next generation. But like any young girl of eighteen, Jenny had been angry when she had discovered what her parents were doing. John was asked to tea almost every Sunday night. John was also asked to come out from town and advise on the sub-clovers or give his opinion as to where the next bore should be sunk. (This last was to provide next season's water for the growing number of horses her father was breeding.)

And on such occasions, her father would invariably remark, "Jenny, you go along with John and show him where we've cross-sticked the likely areas." This would be followed by a kindly smile to John. There would also be a wise-parent expression on his face as he would add: "Jenny knows almost as much about the horses as I do. A real little farmer is our Jenny. You're the expert, John. You ply her with questions and see if she doesn't come up with the right answers every time."

Jenny, at first, had been pleased that her father had so much confidence in her. And mostly, when she went down to the horse paddock with John it was to catch

Redcoat. Then, with her hand on Redcoat's neck, she would lead him to John, who would be sitting on the top rail.

She had no heart or mind for anything else but her beloved favourite, however. To show off Redcoat's paces, she would spring up on his back and ride him round the paddock, bare-backed and at full pace.

She had no idea that she angered John, not only because of her love for the horse but because she would ride him through the bush on off days and always at a great pace.

Repeatedly John had said, "You shouldn't do that, Jenny. One day he'll run you against a tree—Or worse, throw you. He has too much spirit."

"Redcoat throw me? Why, he loves me as much as I love him. He would never hurt me. I know exactly what he's going to do, always. Like he knows me."

But John Downing considered that Jenny's habit of giving the mount his head through virgin bush was something more than foolish. He was a conservative man in all his dealings with animals. After a while Jenny began to realize this. She knew John was a good Pastoral Agent and that he understood bloodstock. But for its *value,* not for love. Never for love.

Then one day she came upon her father and John talking business in the homestead office. She caught the name "Redcoat" but didn't think anything of it at the moment. A week later, home from a visit to a neighbouring farm, she was told that John had sold Redcoat to a pastoralist at a price that Jenny's father declared to be very satisfactory. "A splendid agent is John," her father said pointedly. "Couldn't have fetched a better price at the auction. Knows his horseflesh does John."

Mr. Haseltine was annoyed when he saw the expression on Jenny's face, and the tears in her eyes.

"Now, now. Listen, Jenny," he had said, putting his arm round her shoulders. "There are plenty more three-year-olds coming on. I've always told you not to get too fond of any one animal. I breed them to sell. Sooner or later this favourite or that *must* go up for sale. Besides, John did not like you always riding the one mount. He felt Redcoat could get out of hand, and not fetch a good market price—"

Jenny had slipped from her father's arm and run out of the room.

So John had done it! *John* had sold Redcoat! *John* had planned to do that—when he knew how much she loved Redcoat!

All that had been three weeks ago.

Two days later there had come this advertisement seeking a country-style cook for a safari leaving shortly for the Outback. Jenny had answered it. Her parents had agreed that a period away from the farm would do her good.

The winning of the post had been an uphill job. Any number of girls had applied, including Caroline Holmes, also from Yaraandoo. In fact, Caroline had been selected, though Jenny's old school friend, Geoff Hallam, had put in a good word for her. Then, at the last minute, Caroline had sprung a "query appendix" problem. Geoff had driven up to the farm with the news.

"Come on, Jenny, throw some things in a satchel and jump in. *Now!*" he said. "The fellow doing the advance fitting-out for the safari is back in town. You'll be the first on his doorstep. Just come and take over. Be there—and the job will be yours!"

Geoff had been right.

There had been no time for goodbyes, except to her parents. There'd been hardly time to "throw" her things into a travel bag.

Jenny had spent the rest of that afternoon, and half the night, checking over the stores with Paul Collett, the organizer; and at daybreak she was ready to start off with Geoff in his Land Rover. Paul Collett had gone ahead at midnight and promised to meet up with them somewhere along the old gold-fields road.

How John Downing had learned at such short notice that she was going, Jenny did not know. But he was there to see them off. She supposed someone at home had rung through and told him. So she had tried to be nice to him. In this she was helped by the rising excitement of actually getting away.

It wasn't, therefore, a down-in-the-mouth Jenny who waved goodbye. She was all smiles, her blue-blue eyes shining as she kissed her two sisters and her mother. She didn't even mind the pecks she and John exchanged. She was thinking of other things. Things like the snake of gravel road through forest land till they would reach the Bitumen Highway. And the long roll of blue road three hundred and thirty miles eastwards towards the gold fields.

Now here she was.

It was a lovely bushland morning. The scent of eucalyptus filled the air. Now and again came the faint scampering sound of a wallaby hopping its way through the grey, anonymous bush. Black cockatoos—a flash of red in their wings—chevroned their way to the apple orchards along the west creek.

"So you're all that keen to get away from the homestead nest!" Geoff said thoughtfully, not for the first time. "Ah, well! I'm a bit of a nomad myself, else I wouldn't go tacking myself on to safaris, would I? That makes two of us."

"You helped me get this job, Geoff. I'm grateful." Jenny's lovely, long, black hair was over her shoulder again. She threw it back, fished in her dilly-bag for a piece of ribbon, and tied it up. "As cook and general rouseabout I'll have to remember to keep my hair out of everything, won't I?" she finished with a laugh.

"Yep. Drew Carey's about the tidiest man ever. Has a thing about it. And don't thank me too soon about getting the job. Wait till the Big Boss Fella accepts you. You're not in till he says so."

Jenny made a small grimace. "Don't be so scary, Geoff," she pleaded. "Paul Collett—doing the base organizing—had the authority to find someone, didn't he? I was second choice to Caroline. I mean, I was next on the list, wasn't I?"

"Uh-huh. But I never count my gemstones till I have

them in the bag. So don't get all hepped up, honey. Not till Drew Carey gives the okay."

"Are you being exasperating, Geoff? Or just advising caution?"

"Caution. That's for sure!" Geoff grinned cheerfully.

"We know one another too well," Jenny remarked philosophically. "You can't believe I'm as good a cook as I am. I can't believe you're all that good at motor mechanics."

"I'm a very good mechanic," Geoff said, glancing sideways at her, still wearing a self-satisfied grin. "And Drew Carey knows it. He's had me out on his excursions before."

"And I have yet to be tried out."

"Exactly."

"Paul Collett thinks I'll be all right," she said, hopefully.

"It's his responsibility. Not mine." Geoff was still teasing.

"Would you be pleased if I were sent back?" Jenny asked. "You almost sound like it."

Geoff went on steadily gazing at the track in front of them.

"Not a bit," he said. "How's that for a fair answer?"

Jenny smiled, and the smile grew into a laugh.

"But watch out for Drew Carey all the same," Geoff added. "And don't say I didn't warn you."

He changed gears as they took a gravel hill. He narrowed his eyes now against the shafts of sunlight striking through the leafy treetops. It was an hour after sunup and the jarrah forest was at its best—except for the tantalizing cross-lights between the sapling tree stems.

"Drew's a cagey bird, Jenny," Geoff said quietly. "He leaves the preliminary organization to Paul Collett because he knows Paul doesn't make mistakes. Not ever. Paul does all the groundwork organization for most safaris setting off for the Outback. That's his business. A lucrative one, too. But once he's seen a safari off—and well on its way—he dices out. Leaves the rest

to whoever is running the show. In our case, it's Drew
Carey. Me? I have to stay with it the whole way; so I
can't leave my mistakes behind me this side of the
'scarp."

"You're being sorry for yourself," Jenny said, her
brilliant blue eyes shining with fun now. Then she became serious again. "But what is he really like, this
Drew Carey?"

"He's okay, Jenny. But don't forget he's the boss.
He'll turf you out as soon as look at you, if you make
more than one mistake."

"I shan't make even *one* mistake," Jenny said, tilting
her chin. She was being very resolute now and showing
it.

"Half your luck," Geoff said. "You must be more
than human."

"No. Just conscientious."

"Don't turn out to be a second Nicole, honey. That's
the only boon I ask."

"Nicole?"

Geoff shrugged. "His co-partner. A bit too settled in
to call her a mere girl friend. She's very close to him! I
met her on one of Drew's safaris last year. She's a real
looker. The kind you think you'll never meet till one
day you do. Straight out of the top bracket. She's supposed to have a mighty bank account, and collects
gemstones in her own right. Happens to be very know-
all about the ghost towns. You taking all this in,
Jenny?"

She nodded. "Every word," she said.

"Nicole was born Outback," Geoff went on. "Her father had something to do with the Sons of Gwalia mine
in the old gold-boom days. He owned land, too. Was
partner in a sheep station a but further Outback. Anyhow, there isn't much Nicole doesn't know about the
whole area. She has a reputation for not being able to
keep away from the place—once she has a chance to
get out of town."

"Well," said Jenny judicially. "To me she sounds
like a very capable as well as attractive sort of person."

Geoff laughed. He slowed the Rover down to let an emu stroll across the road. "That bird will really get the bird one day," he said balefully. "What with kangaroos and emus, life can be very hazardous out this way."

"I think they're gorgeous. Especially the kangaroos."

"Yes. But you're not driving," Geoff said. "If I clobber one of those, my conscience *and* the conservationists will be after me. That is, if I'm still alive under a bowled-out car. Just remember, when you take over the driving, to watch what's moving in the bush alongside you. If it's either kangaroo or emu, it's ten to one it'll start crossing the road without giving reasonable attention to old *homo sapiens*. You'll be lucky to stay alive and whole."

"I'll remember," Jenny said. "Don't forget we have the 'roos around Yaraandoo, too."

"Not like you have them up here. They get more and more numerous the nearer you get to the Outback."

Jenny unwound her arms from her knees. "You were telling me about Nicole," she said reproachfully.

"Like I said, she has everything. Including good looks, property, and money."

"So everyone's rich except you and me," Jenny said, with mock sadness. She pushed her wandering hair back over her shoulder again. "Do you or don't you like her, Geoff?"

"I like her as a matter of policy. I don't get in Drew's shadow, though. She's too high-powered for me. She's all Drew's for the duration! But I have to be honest. I'd like her better if only she wasn't so dedicated to getting her own way most of the time!"

"Her own way?" Jenny echoed, "But I thought Drew Carey was very much the big boss?"

"So he is. That makes two of them, doesn't it?"

Jenny puckered her brow and did some thinking. "In that case," she said slowly, "in that case, there being two bosses—they must *act* as one. Two people acting as one generally means—"

Geoff nodded. "That's right! So mind your p's and

q's, angel. Like I said, there isn't anything Nicole doesn't know about the old gold fields. And that's where we're heading now. Drew's after more gemstones for his collection. So he says, anyway. Mostly *opal*. Hurrah for *opal*! Nicole is along to keep her eye on Drew, as well as watch out for marauders around the old ghost towns."

"They said on TV that Drew Carey has the best and most valuable gem collection in Australia. How does he know where to go looking for such things?"

"He has his watchdogs out. On full pay, too. Old prospectors mostly. A few hermits living out their lives in the Outback. They're small-time gem operators who want to sell, and not collect. They make a living that way. You name them, Drew has them on his visiting list."

Jenny was thoughtful for quite sixty seconds. "What bothers me is, how does he pay them if they're right Outback? Does he go loaded down with dollars? That would be dangerous now that the highway men are back on the road, thanks to the mining boom."

"Drew get stood up by modern-day bushrangers? He has trading posts. Only he and his clients know where they are." Geoff's voice turned mock-sepulchral. "Watch out, for one dark night Drew will away to make a deal. In the small, light hours before sunup, his step will be heard wending its homeward way back to the camp—minus dollars, but heavy with opal, or whatever he's after!"

Jenny burst out laughing. Her eyes shone, and her beautiful white teeth flashed.

"Oh Geoff," she said, "you *are* joking."

He gave her an indignant look. "Okay!" he said, very superior now. "Just you wait and see. And don't say I didn't warn you. Bushrangers are for real—this very day and age! They may look as if they're just followers. But that's only a fancy, three-syllable word meaning 'spy'—someone who wants to see what you're up to in the money game. And Drew Carey knows it. I tell you, Jenny—he's nobody's fool!"

2

"The maree forest's all in flower," Jenny said, looking at the great trees as the Rover swung into a by-track. "The beehives will be out, and the honey flow will start. Funny how one can always tell when winter is gone. There are white flowers in the crowns of those gum trees."

"Changing the subject, hey?"

"Changing the subject," Jenny agreed. She wasn't sure she wanted to hear more about those bushrangers anyway. She knew that one or two of them—modern-day and in cars—had prowled the Nullabor Plain. There had been *deaths*.

And she did love the giant maree trees with their creamy flowers and their drone of bees. Better think of these things! She loved the undergrowth, thick with low-growing bushes—some prickly, yet sweet-smelling in an earthy way. It was so still, as if every tree, every bush, was waiting for something. And watching. It was strange—that waiting watchfulness of the bush. What did it mean? Yet *it* wasn't frightening.

"Why so silent?" Geoff asked suddenly. "Still dreaming your last farewells with John-o. Homesick already?"

"No, I'm not homesick. No, I'm not thinking of anyone in particular. And please don't call him John-o. No one else does. So why have you taken to calling him that, all of a sudden?"

"Up in arms in defence, hey?"

"He's a friend, in a way. You'd defend a friend, wouldn't you?"

"With both fists. But then I'm not likely to be in love with someone you took to with fists, am I?"

Tha's what's wrong with me. That's the trouble, Jenny thought. I'm not in love with John. That's what's wrong with me.

"Oh, bother, bother!" she said aloud, and wiped the back of her hand across her eyes.

"Hey, what goes?" Geoff asked. "Dust in your eyes?"

"Yes. Dust in my eyes." Jenny felt guilty. "It's all right now," she added. "When will we reach Northam?"

"Soon enough. We're halfway up the Darling 'Scarp now. Next we go through a stretch of farm land. This road will take us eastways to the main gold-fields line." He glanced down at her. "And the Big Boss Fella!" he added heavily. "I'd better stick around to warn Drew we've taken on a different girl from the one he expects. You'll need protecting."

"For goodness-sake, why? If Caroline hadn't applied for this job I'd have it anyway, wouldn't I?"

"Yep. But Caroline, plus all that flattering report on her, is what Big Boss Fella is *expecting*. How about changing your name for the duration?"

"I could, but I won't." Jenny was firm about this. "I've already given my forwarding address to my parents. It would look very peculiar for someone called 'Caroline,' to be collecting mail for someone called 'Jenny,' wouldn't it?"

"Badly peculiar," Geoff amended. "All the mail for this outfit will go into Denong Outpost Mail Bag and will be handed over to Drew Carey. And to none other."

I'll be myself! For the first time in my life! I'm completely free! Jenny went on thinking.

She wanted to sing the message to the treetops and to the grassy grazing paddocks they were passing.

For although she might appear to be only a girl sitting in the passenger seat of a Land Rover, in spirit Jenny was someone on top of the world. Once over the

Darling Escarpment she would be heading towards wattle country, and the Outback. Towards wonderland!

Funny how it all had happened so quickly, she thought. Then she stopped thinking because there, at the entrance to a roadhouse, was Paul Collett's Rover. And alongside it stood a much bigger vehicle. A land Cruiser—with caravan and trailer linked on behind! Two men stood watching them drive up through a pall of dust. Jenny recognized Paul at once. She was lifting her hand to wave when she realized the other man might be the Big Boss Fella, Drew Carey.

Geoff slowed to a stop and opened the door. Jenny sat still now, feeling anxious that she had at last to meet the Big Man. He was tall and rangy like Paul, only more so. But there was something striking about the way he stood. He was not only different from Paul and Geoff, but from anyone else she knew. His stillness was almost statue-like; yet she knew instinctively that when he did move, it would be very meaningful. And there was a sort of concealed alertness about him as he looked over the short distance towards Geoff's Land Rover from under a broad-brimmed Outbacker's hat. He was both aware and quiet—in some significant way Jenny could not define.

His khaki shorts and shirt exactly suited the burned brownness of his face, his arms, and—yes—his hands.

He moved towards them now. No gesture of his was aimless or wasted. He lifted his hat fractionally, replaced it on his head, then said in a low voice, almost a drawl, "Good day, Geoff! I see you've arrived in good time. And this is . . .?" His grey-blue eyes rested on Jenny. He did not finish the question but waited for Geoff to explain. There was no expression at all in those guarded eyes now.

"Jenny Haseltine," Geoff said. "The other girl became ill. I guess Paul let you know about it."

"Good morning, Jenny. We use given names on the safari, always. I hope you understand?" He was looking directly at her. The anxiety she felt was because Geoff, sitting beside her, was no doubt hiding a grin at her expense. He *knew* she was suddenly nervous, all on account of being impressed by this tall, quiet man who was to be her boss.

"G'day, Drew," Geoff said casually. "As you see, I've brought the goods, as well as the girl!

Paul had come across himself, and opened the door for Jenny. She dropped to the ground without waiting for him to give her his hand.

"Hallo, Paul," she said, her smile switching on and off from sheer nervousness. "I'm here, as Geoff said. Safe and sound."

Paul smiled kindly. "In wind, limb, and enthusiasm?" he asked kindly.

"All three." She went on smiling, rather crookedly. She glanced past him to see how Drew Carey was taking her in. She was disconcerted because he didn't seem to be taking her in at all. He had given her one glance, lifted his Outbacker's hat with a casual gesture, then turned to Geoff.

"You picked up all the stores, Geoff? And checked them item by item?" he asked.

Jenny had to admit he had a good voice. It was soft, yet somehow carried authority.

Oh dear! Jenny thought ruefully. She wasn't used to being ignored quite as much as this. She was a country girl from a small country town where everyone knew her and where everyone—but *everyone*—said, "Hallo, Jenny. How goes it?" and *smiled,* even if she was flying past in one of her top-speed hurries.

She was impressed by Drew Carey, but wasn't sure she was going to like him. Well, she'd wait and see. She had to hide her reservations, of course. She *did* want to keep her job.

Drew pulled his hat down over his brow, shading his eyes as he looked beyond Jenny into the far reaches of the bushland. There was quite a silence.

The bush was silent too, as if it, too, was affected by this quite, deliberate man.

"Which name . . .?" he began. Then he glanced from

Geoff back to Jenny, as if waiting for someone to en-
lighten him.

"Jenny Haseltine," Paul Collett explained, coming
round the Rover at that moment.

"How do you do, Miss——. *Which* name did you
say?"

"Just Jenny!" she said, blinking a little from sheer
nervousness. She lifted her chin a good inch and looked
directly at Drew. She knew she had to kill that unexpected bout of nerves. She tried a small smile, just to
see how that worked.

He had a strong-featured face, she thought. His grey
eyes—with a hint of blue in them—were very clear.
Disconcertingly so. She knew her own expression must
not waver. He had to have confidence in her, didn't he?

"Thank you for filling our vacancy," he said unexpectedly. "I'm sure you will take the place of the other
girl quite adequately." He did not smile. Yet there was
something about his face, and his eyes, that was as
good as a smile to her.

Jenny's heart suddenly warmed. She felt a new and
strange excitement stirring somewhere inside her. She
would have liked to make a small speech about being
glad to come—willing and able and all that. But she
didn't think she could trust her voice. So she just swallowed hard and smiled. Her smile was lovely. But she
couldn't see it; so she didn't know it. Geoff, from a safe
position one foot behind Drew's left shoulder, winked
at her. Drew turned on his heel at that moment and
saw him. His eyebrows went up but he said nothing.

Jenny didn't wink back. She knew Geoff was having
the time of his life watching her grapple with her new
boss.

Drew Carey turned to Paul again. "If you wouldn't
mind doing a check over Geoff's stores before you
leave, Paul. We'll do our best to make an early start.
You know where to pick up Nicole? And you know the
date for meeting up with us when we finish at the opal
pads? If we decide, by any change of plan, to go north

through the ghost towns you'll get the message through Denong Outpost. All clear?"

"As daylight," Paul said. "Come on, Geoff, let's check over your gear."

"Anyone would think I hadn't checked myself," Geoff growled as they moved off, but not so loudly that Drew could hear him.

"You know that Drew invariably does a double check," Paul said placatingly, "especially of breakdown duplicate parts for the vehicles. You've been with him before, Geoff."

The two men were moving to the rear of Geoff's Land Rover. Drew glanced over his shoulder as he walked away. Jenny saw the flash of a clever, almost indulgent smile in his eyes as he looked at the other two men. It had the unexpected effect of a winged message for Jenny. The Big Boss Fella knew all about his men—both inside and out. It amused him to see them doing exactly what he wanted them to do: Geoff putting up a defensive grumble, Paul acting as the pipe line between Geoff and himself.

Jenny straightened her shoulders as she took in a breath. She hoped that Drew wouldn't play her like a fish. Because that, in an infinitesimal way, was what he was doing right now with that glance over his shoulder. She would watch out. She had learned two things about him already. He could be very firm, very brief with his smiles; and the grey-blue eyes took in everything and missed nothing of what was going on around him. Even when his back was turned.

Watch out, Jenny, she warned herself. Whatever you do or whatever you say, somewhere he's noting it and notching it up—for, or against. For future reference.

She wasn't so sure she liked him at all now. He was very impressive. Oh yes! But she didn't want to have a chill down her spine every time *her* back was turned.

Three-quarters of an hour later, the stores double-checked and a last conference with Drew finished, Paul Collett left them. He was heading back towards the coast to start off the next safari on his list. He would meet up with them again at some later date.

Jenny ran over to his car as he started up the engine. She wanted to thank him once again for getting her this job.

He shook his head as he smiled at her. "Not so! You got yourself the job, Jenny. Just by being yourself. Stay that way. Right?"

"I'll try," she said. "But thank you. I won't let you down."

"Whoever thought you would?" He smiled at her as he raced the engine of his car, then changed gear and moved forward. The last Jenny saw of him was a wave of his right hand and the dust cloud thrown up as his car moved off.

He really is a nice man! Jenny thought to herself. She wished he'd come back to join them soon. Very soon.

She was so preoccupied with watching the last of Paul's dust disappear over a rise that she didn't see Drew Carey come across the stretch of gravel towards her.

"Miss Haseltine," he said as she turned round. "Jenny. You don't mind first names? As I have already told you, we all use the given name while on safari."

Jenny nodded. There had been a little grief in her heart now that Paul Collett was gone, but this same grief was jolted completely out of sight by Drew's presence.

"Right. Jenny it is!" he said. "What I've come to ask you is, have you any experience of driving a Land Rover?"

"Yes," she said. "I drive our Rover on the farm. An old creaky one, I'm afraid."

"You can handle the gears?" He was looking at her hands. They were fine, slim-boned hands, but they were strong. They had become that way not only from driving the Land Rover but also from handling horses—even those newly broken in.

"Yes. No trouble at all," she said.

"Okay. Then take Geoff's Rover, will you? I'm taking Geoff along with me for the next few miles. We've altered some of our plans and this is the best chance of talking them over. I want to save time. I might drive fairly fast, as we're already somewhat late. Follow my dust. Speed up any time you look like losing it. Okay?"

"Yes. Quite clear. You want me to fix my distance from you, then keep you in sight."

He nearly smiled, but not quite.

"Yes. As near as possible," was all he said.

Jenny was quite sure that, as he walked back to his own outfit, he was having a quiet think-about at her expense. She was afraid she had answered like a private on parade. She now felt angry with herself. Oh well, he couldn't say she wasn't trying.

Geoff came across the gravel patch to say "Cheers, and goodbye."

"Sorry to leave you," he said, and patted her shoulder. "Drew wants to talk business as he drives. What's eating him is that he doesn't want to keep our so-called navigator—meaning Nicole—waiting. He's a sort of punctual guy always, but doubles up when he has to catch up with that dame. Watch the oil gauge, will you, luv? This one-fella Rover is a devil for chewing up oil. That's why it smokes behind, even on the bitumen."

"I'll watch it," Jenny said. "I know where you keep the oil, and what's more important, I know where and how to oil this tin can anyway."

"Call my Rover a tin can?" Geoff exclaimed with indignation. "I'll write to the makers about you. You'll get a stinger from them!"

"Overseas mail?" said Jenny. "Well, that will be a change from home chat, anyway."

"All depends what the 'home chat' is like," Geoff said with a grin. "Can't see old John-o pasting his heart on a bit of paper."

"*Don't* call him 'John-o'," Jenny said firmly, not for the first time. She was very serious now. "His name is plain John. And if he *has* a heart, I wouldn't know."

"Okay, okay, okay! He's 'plain John.' Does he know you call him that?"

"I don't know. It's just that he's not here to speak for himself. That's not fair, is it?"

"Nope. Except that all's fair in love or war. Which is it, honey? Love or war?"

Jenny longed to say "neither" very sharply. But that would be an open invitation for Geoff to go on teasing her.

"Hoi there, Geoff!" Drew had turned, and was looking back at them. "You coming or getting sacked? I'm waiting."

Geoff winked at Jenny, then strode off towards Drew. Jenny hoisted herself into the Land Rover and turned the ignition key. With the gear in neutral but her foot clear of the accelerator, she ran the gear stick through its routine. It wasn't even stiff. Hurray for Geoff, she thought, more kindly disposed to him now. He can be thorough when he likes. It's almost too easy.

She sat, her hands on the steering wheel, watching through the windscreen as Geoff and Drew hoisted themselves into the Land Cruiser and started up. It was quite an outfit! Land Cruiser, caravan, and trailer with a large "Over Length" notice in front and at the rear! She watched them move off, edging on to the road and beginning to gather speed as they went ahead. Still she did not move. She knew what that old rule "Follow my dust" meant. One had to keep one's distance from the vehicle in front. You should be far enough not to be able to see the vehicle, yet near enough to see its dust. Too close behind and the dust could blind you. Down south in her home town, drivers had to keep five car lengths behind the car in front. Right Outback they might need to be a quarter of a mile apart. The dust thrown up by a moving vehicle in these areas could hang like a blinding cloud for minutes after that same vehicle had passed through.

3

An hour later they turned off the bitumen and took a cross track northwards towards the distant claypan country. Far to the west Jenny could see a line of paperbark trees. Here and there a giant river gum towered above them.

The upper reaches of the river, she thought. We must be heading for the Roadhouse at Wooragong. There's nothing else on the map this way.

Driving at the same speed as Drew—now a long distance in front—and watching his dust cloud, Jenny fell to thinking of Nicole, who knew the backtracks and byways through to the Outback. Nicole must really be something special. Drew Carey would certainly be careful about his choice of a navigator. And usually it was a man, wasn't it? For the navigator had to be able to guide the driver over wastelands, across certain claypans, and *not* across others. It had to be someone who knew every bend of the track and every notch on every black stump—all those things that were the landmarks. As for Nicole's vaunted "beauty"—beauty could mean anything, Jenny thought curiously of this important "navigator." One man's liking could be something another man didn't care about. Otherwise all the men would want to marry the same person, wouldn't they?

Now if John had come along, he might have fallen for Nicole, too. That would leave Jenny herself free to bury her conscience. She would be free like the things that rustled and scampered in the bush all around. Like the black cockatoos in the sky.

Thinking of John made her unhappy again. She was

well behind Drew's dust cloud so it couldn't be the dust that suddenly made her eyes smart. Yet why was there something, when thinking of John, that hurt her? It had to be a nasty prickle of guilt. Everyone in Yaraandoo had made a couple of herself and John. And so now she mustn't make a fool of him. Or of herself. But the only way to make a break was for one of them not to be there. Then time and distance would work their alchemy. At least Jenny hoped that was how it would be. Happy ever after? Was anyone ever really happy ever after when there weren't any rainbows in the sky?

All right. So she'd run away! And now her eyes smarted. So what?

The gravel track widened and splayed out south to let another track join it. Suddenly Drew's dust cloud came to a standstill, then gradually disintegrated and spread itself into a low, brown, misty death through the bush on either side.

With a clear view at last, Jenny could see the tree-shaded Wooragong Roadhouse.

Beside the roadhouse was a Mercedes Benz and beside that, two feet away, Drew's outfit had come to a halt.

Geoff was wandering round the caravan trailer, kicking the tires with his boot as if not wanting at the moment to intrude in the goings-on a few yards away. Drew—out of his seat—was being warmly embraced by a young woman. She was tall, slim, and neatly dressed in a tailored safari outfit. At this minute she was very busy gazing into Drew's face.

She took no notice of Jenny's Rover slowing to a stop on the down side of the track.

Geoff strolled across to Jenny. "So you made it!" he said, pretending surprise. "You missed all the black stumps, didn't glue yourself in a single claypan, and by the notable absence of dents in your 'roo bars you didn't hit any kangaroos."

"I didn't even *see* one," Jenny said loftily. "I was doing what I was told to do—watching Drew's dust."

"Obeying the boss? Good girl! By the look of what's

going on over yonder—halfway between the outfit and that ostentatious Mercedes Benz—you're likely to see two bosses who'll direct you from now on instead of merely one. How you going to like that, Jen?"

"I might like her. And if I do, I might even like having two bosses. Who knows? Don't forget you're in the same spot yourself, Geoff."

"Well, if they keep up that heart-to-heart much longer we—that's you and me—might take an example from them and start one of our own."

He grinned cheerfully. Jenny laughed back.

"That'll be the day!" she said. "The fighting's over for us, and the loving is on? Is that what you mean?"

"Well, nearly. But not till I've blown all thoughts of John Downing out of my mind. Not to mention what's going on in *your* mind, pet. Just how deep *is* that well of affection you've stored up for 'plain John' back home?"

Jenny didn't have time to reply. Drew and his fine lady had finished their marathon greeting, and had turned towards them.

"Hoi, Geoff!" Drew called. "Bring Jenny over, will you? She must meet Nicole."

"My, oh my!" Geoff said, half under his breath. "Look how she's captured his arm. She's not going to let you jump *her* gates, Jenny girl."

"I wouldn't *want* to jump any gates," Jenny said lightly. "And I haven't any right to worry about who is hanging on to his arm, have I? In spite of the fright-making things you said about him, Geoff, he *is* rather nice."

"So I didn't scare you off? Well, well! He hasn't shown tooth and claw yet, honey. But there's time aplenty ahead."

They had reached that narrow space between the dusty Mercedes and the Land Cruiser. For all her curiosity about Nicole, Jenny found herself looking at Drew first. Those eyes, mostly grey now, were smiling at her; yet his mouth did *not*. Curiouser and curiouser, she thought. She wanted to know if, in his estimation, she had driven the Land Rover to rule. She wished, if she'd come up to standard, he would say so.

"No dust in your eyes, Jenny?" he asked.

Was it the unexpected *something* in his voice, or was it her guilt prickles again? She simply couldn't answer him. There *had* been things in her eyes that were not particles of dust; yet she couldn't say so. But if he'd been that nasty bullying Boss Fella of whom Geoff had spoken, she wouldn't feel so embarassed now. He wasn't—at this moment, anyway—like that at all!

She shook her head and glanced at Nicole, who still kept her hand on Drew's arm.

She really is a stunner! Jenny thought, with a twinge of envy. Nicole had the kind of skin that burned to a lovely smooth tan. Her eyes were green, dark-fringed, and very unusual. They were full of light and intelligence—and a certain watchfulness. Jenny wondered if her own face was dusty or her hair disarrayed.

"This is Jenny Haseltine. Cook, bottle-washer, and general rouseabout, Nicole," Drew said formally. "Jenny, this is Nicole Armstrong." His smile had a touch of wry amusement about it as he added: "Nicole, you have met Geoff Hallam before. He was in the team when we cut into the Warburton Ranges. Remember?"

Nicole nodded. "Of course. He did very well cleaning up the car engines after we came through that strip of sand-dune country. I remember *that*—quite well."

She had a good voice too, Jenny thought. It has just the right amount of matter-of-factness in it.

Geoff gave his most aimless smile. He had a certain respect for Nicole. She was a person who knew the highways, byways, claypans, buttes, gnamma holes, salt grass, and spinifex that spelled the part of the Outback for which they were now destined.

"You were with us three weeks and five days," Nicole went on.

"You have a mind like a calendar," Geoff said, blinking—clearly in admiration for the exactitude with which she remembered the "three weeks and five days."

"It works like clockwork, too,'" she commented flatly.

Geoff ran his forefinger down the line of his jawbone and shook his head. He was registering, not for the first time, that this beautiful person could outwit him in what had been solely his realm to date—the world of back-chat talk.

Jenny looked over the low, grey wilderness of the bushland hereabouts, then back to Drew Carey again.

He was not following the conversation between Nicole and Geoff. He had glanced first at the sun, then at the shadows on the ground. Then he looked at his wrist watch.

"Do you agree it's wise to make a run for Coolgardie, Nicole?" It was more a statement than a question.

"We can take a short cut through Appleyard's back paddock to the bitumen," she replied, again with that touch of matter-of-factness in her voice. "That is—" she paused and looked Jenny over—"*if* our cook and bottle-washer can drive the Land Rover through scrub patches. If not, Geoff should take over the driving. She could go along with him, of course."

"Jenny?" Drew looked at her. His eyes could be kind, but they weren't just now. They were asking a question and nothing more.

"I can carry on with the Rover," Jenny said firmly. "I'm used to driving through bushland by day. By night, too, when it's time for moonlight seeding. But if Geoff could come along with me, it would be company."

Drew actually smiled. It was a mere flash, but it had something curious yet special in it. He glanced at Geoff.

"Geoff, you swap over and partner Jenny, will you?" he said. "I'll accompany Nicole. We need to drill over the plans again. You might give Jenny a rough outline of them, too, while you're with her. We'll each one of us then be more or less informed as to our immediate future movements. All agreed?"

He took out a cigarette and lit it, then glanced round the circle.

Jenny thought how clever he was, behind that facade of quiet good manners. He really *was* the Big Boss Fella, but he made each one think he or she was being consulted in the making of decisions. Was there a small touch of cunning about him? Kind in manner, soft in speech. Nice eyes that beguiled, but might be part of the facade. She would ask him, when she had the chance, if he played chess. That kind of approach to people generally indicated that they were no more important than pawns. It was true that Drew seemed to play his pawns as gently, thoughtfully, and carefully as any man might who always *meant to win.*

But then the Big Boss Fella of a safari needed to win, didn't he? He was the responsible one.

Oh, dear! What an enigma he was turning out to be!

4

"Geoff," Jenny said when they were at last in the Land Rover. (This time she was in the passenger seat.) She thought she too might play Drew's strategy game; she would defer to Geoff's manly superiority. Just to keep the peace. "Geoff? Why did you not say that our navigator was married? Or a widow? Or something? She has a gold ring on her fourth finger. But Drew called her *Miss* Armstrong."

"That's what she calls herself," Geoff said, narrowing his eyes to see through the bush shadows as he swung the Land Rover around to make a half-circle turn in the track.

"But why?"

"She prefers it. In actual fact, she's a sort of grass widow. First she marries, then she quits. Now she's gone back to base. Meaning she's become a 'Miss' again."

"How long ago?"

"Just after the Warburton Range trip. But judging from that arm-holding, eye-gazing routine we witnessed a while back, I would guess that maybe she really has herself a hang-up on Drew. You pulled in three minutes too late, Jenny, to see the arms-round-the-neck connection that went on at their reunion."

He glanced at her. His grin was puckish. "Adds to her glamour, don't you think? The 'Miss' who was once a 'Missus.' Food for thought, hey?"

"Well—it *is* her affair, isn't it?"

"Which affair? The one when she was a 'Missus' or the one now she's back to 'Miss'?"

25

"Both," Jenny said firmly, and turned her head to look at the landscape. She wondered why it bothered her that Nicole had once been married, and now wasn't.

The galahs in the grey-and-pink cloud-blur of homeward flight were winging across the bush in a massive formation. There were hundreds of them.

"Oh! Aren't they *beautiful?*" Jenny exclaimed, meaning the galahs. She eased down in her seat, rested one arm on the open window frame, and gave herself up to bird-watching. She wished she had not been so curious about Nicole. Lesson one, she thought. I came away to see the bush and the bees, the kangaroos, the emus, and all things *free.* Not people who were tied, or untied, or just *trying.* Oh, dear! There I go thinking about Nicole and Drew again!

To make amends she had to think and say something nice.

"What a mind she has!" she said aloud, still watching the last of the galahs disappear over the distant trees. "Imagine remembering it wasn't one month but was exactly three weeks and five days. After all that time, too."

"Not so much her mind as my fascinating personality," Geoff said grimly. "That is by reputation, of course. Even in her dreams she was counting the days lost out of a lifetime of what might have been a great partnership."

Jenny looked at Geoff's profile. She was puzzled.

"What are you talking about? A great partnership? Do you mean fun or love?"

"Neither. I'm being brave about money. Much the most important thing. She has loads of it. I had great schemes schemed out to beguile her into a wonderful partnership. She would pay out the costs—and I would collect the fame. It was all to do with the ghost towns of the old gold-fields belt, this side of the border country. Did you know the world price of gold is going up and up, Jenny? And someone is going to make a packet out of all the gold in them thar mullock heaps round all the derelict mines north of the Esperance Plains?"

"And your scheme was to stake the claims? Maybe find the gold? And Nicole would pay the excursion costs?"

"How good you are at guessing right! Except we call it safari nowadays. More sophisticated. Covers a lot of things—such as moonlighting on someone else's pegging claim as well as establishing claims of one's own. It all requires enterprise, physical work. But mostly *money*."

Jenny did not laugh this time. A horrid thought had crossed her mind.

Were Nicole Armstrong and Drew Carey in such a partnership? Did this safari—now—have the same skeleton plan? Drew's enterprise was nominally a hunt through the old opal pads. He was apparently only a gem collector, scouting the field. But was all this merely a cover for some other activities?

Opals, some few of them, had been found north of Kalgoorlie, as well as south of Coolgardie in the long-time back. An interesting strike had been made east of Kalgoorlie just recently. And Nicole Armstrong was interested in gemstones, too! They were all over, everywhere—just waiting to be picked up! But gold? That was something different! It cost big, very big money to get gold out of the wilderness.

Geoff's eyes were reading her thoughts.

"It's deep down, the precious stuff," he said. "Not lying about on the ridges. So it costs plenty to get it out."

For some strange reason Jenny didn't feel so bright and gay as she had meant to feel. She actually felt—ever so slightly—depressed.

They spent that night at one of the more modern roadhouses on the east fringes of the wattle country, apparently built especially for guests on safari.

These safaris, some equipped and planned by Paul Collett, were all the go these days, it seemed. Groups trekked north to see the Ord River in flood, or east to discover what went with the nickel boom. But some safari-goers were more shadowy in their hithering and thithering. Posing as tourists, they were really bent on meeting up with lone prospectors. Any one of these experienced lone prospectors just might turn up the world's biggest emerald, or spot the place where a big, rich company was covertly on the dig for uranium along the surveyed acquifers. In fact, Paul had built himself an overnight business organizing such safaris, now that the mineral boom was on.

"At least every second crew you'll meet," he had once told Geoff, "will be either conservationists on the march, or covert outrunners from some multi-million-dollar mining company who are investigating pegged claims the lesser prospectors now want to sell for hard cash. On the spot, too."

"Yes." Geoff had shrugged. "I've read about it, heard about it, and even seen it on TV."

But Paul had also reassured Jenny about Drew's safari when he had lured her in Caroline's place. "Drew's genuinely and professionally keen on opals. He's got the best gemstone collection this side of the black stump."

"Which black stump?" Jenny had asked with a smile. "There must be a billion of them in the Outback."

"Just a saying!" Paul had said lightly. It can mean anything, anywhere, you know."

"Yes, I know. I didn't mean to be sceptical."

"Well, take care, he had said. Keep your head cool when in a bad spot, and you'll have a wonderfully interesting time."

A bad spot? She remembered his words only now. Why should she ever be in a bad spot? Certainly not with Geoff and Drew around. That bushranger talk again!

The roadhouse sat there on the edge of the Never Never, modern, bright, and comfortable—a benefit from the mining boom.

Beyond the front entrance, the reception desk was

planted alongside a minature bar. The bedrooms ran side by side, each with its own entrance, in a straight line down the side of the main building. Generally travellers had to share because there were more and more travellers coming this way. And building accommodations could not keep up with the new adventure-type holidays.

Drew booked the party in, signing all the names himself to save the manager's time. This potentate—for that was the manager's manner—was also on demand for serving drinks from the bar to other travellers who were not stopping over. The only precaution he took against the possibility of a cheque bouncing was to take down the registration numbers of all vehicles.

Having completed his chores, Drew turned and handed a key to Nicole.

"Number eleven is for you and Jenny," he said. "Geoff and I will be next door in Number twelve. Give us all half an hour to shower and change, then come in for drinks before dinner. Okay?"

Jenny noticed that he smiled at Nicole as he spoke, as if this having drinks together was a routine. As he did not look at Jenny at all, she wasn't sure whether she, too, was included in the invitation.

Ah, well! In thirty minutes time she would know for sure. She felt uneasy about this first exercise in sharing with Nicole, but guessed they had weeks of this situation before them. She would have to get used to it, and learn to like it.

"This way!" Nicole said, passing Jenny but not looking at her. Instead, she glanced over her shoulder and smiled at Drew. For some reason that smile stabbed at Jenny. For the life of her she couldn't think why.

Maybe it was because that smile was so sophisticated, in a possessive kind of way.

Geoff, for his part, winked at Jenny. This said a great deal.

Jenny gave the faintest nod of her head to let Geoff know she'd caught his message. Unfortunately Drew saw it. He looked at her in a steady, thoughtful, un-smiling way.

If only he didn't have those eyes, she thought. She really felt like crawling under a stone or something.

"Well, we'll meet at dinner, I suppose," she said lamely.

"If that is the way you prefer it," Drew answered. "However—" He paused.

Jenny hung on that "however." Was he specifically going to invite *her* for the pre-dinner drinks, too? She was unable to meet his eyes; so she half-turned and watched Nicole go through the entrance door as if she owned the place.

"We do have lemonade, as well as other drinks," Drew said, his eyes still watching Jenny. She thought, but wasn't sure, they had a hint of amusement in them.

He thinks I'm a child, she thought. Then she said aloud, but with a smile: "I'm eighteen. Old enough to vote."

"Yes, of course. Then we could make it a shandy, couldn't we?"

Was he being sarcastic? Nothing showed in his eyes now. They were just watchful, still looking at her steadily.

This man is getting under my skin, Jenny thought. She wanted to toss her hair over her shoulder, a semi-conscious way of demonstrating independence. But caution stopped her in the nick of time. After all, he *was* the Big Boss Fella!

"Thank you. That would be very nice," she said quietly. Too quietly, for she saw at once, though his expression did not alter by a flicker, that he was seeing through her. She also knew that behind his left shoulder Geoff was having a laughing time of it, all at *her* expense.

"Thank you," she said again. She had to conjure up her will power in order to turn with a reasonable amount of dignity and follow Nicole through the doorway to Number eleven.

She walked firmly down the cement pathway under the branches of two gum trees, glancing at the numbered doors as she went and refusing to bite her lips.

I'll be *myself!* she thought with firmness. That's why I came away. To be myself. And instead, I have been behaving like a cuckoo!

She ran the last few yards to stir herself back into form—the always-in-a-hurry girl of Yaraandoo. Was she doomed always to be running away from a man? First John, and now the Big Boss Fella? What did they do to her? Was there something wrong with her?

The key was in the lock of Number eleven. As she put her hand up to turn the key, she thought of Geoff—with relief. She'd never run away from Geoff. She'd charge in first, head down. Somehow that thought restored her confidence.

She turned the key and opened the door.

Now to face Miss Nicole Armstrong! What strategy shall I use? she asked herself—and suddenly realized that strategy was what that Mr. Drew Carey with his much too nice eyes was using on her! He was keeping her nicely docile by wearing an expression that could neither be pinned down nor complained against. From long experience with lots of females, he'd probably found that being charming in an absent sort of way undermined female resistance. Ah, well! She'd just have to watch herself. And him, too!

5

Nicole was already stripped off and slipping into the shower alcove. Jenny, coming in, heard the taps turned on.

"Hallo!" Jenny called brightly over the sound of cascading water.

"Hallo yourself!" Nicole's voice came back. "I'll be ten minutes. I like a good rundown after overlanding. You may have the bed by the window."

"Oh, thank you." Jenny's spirits rose. She always supposed the window bed was the choice one and that Nicole would—by manner and superiority, age and beauty—have taken it for herself.

"Don't thank me," Nicole's half-drowned voice came back through the curtain of water. "I insist on the window being wide open at night. And this time of the year there's an early-morning cold wind from the southeast. Straight through that window. I'm not being unselfish."

Jenny sat down on the bed and laughed. Nicole's candour retorted her spirits. If Nicole was a person who always intended to be herself—loud and clear— then she, Jenny, needn't have guilt feelings about wanting to be herself, too.

Maybe, after all, they were two of a kind.

Nicole emerged from the shower wrapped in a towel, and Jenny—likewise wrapped—darted in. Time was passing and Nicole had been not ten minutes but a quarter of an hour. Drew had only given them half an hour. Jenny was a little taken aback when Nicole called to her to "Hurry up!" Her own long session under the shower had left Jenny little time for both bath *and* dressing.

"Shall try!" she called back, turning the taps on full cock and drowning all chances of further conversation for the next few minutes.

When she did emerge, Nicole was already in a charming, fitted dress that had the twin magic of being both Outbackish yet modish at the same time.

"Oh!" Jenny said. "I don't think I have anything as glamorous as that!"

"Nothing unusual." Nicole's voice was just a little bit airy as she glanced down at her dress. It was made of some pale pink material that had a lovely, soft sheen. Round the neckline there was a two-inch band of glittering spangles. Except for a number of rings on her hands, the spangle band was her only ornament. The dress was beautiful and enhanced her slim figure. Jenny knew instinctively it was the cut of the dress, its simplicity, and the probable cost of the material that made it look so smart. It was faultless—even for the Outback. And it was the sort of dress that could be worn on any occasion with equal effect.

Genius! Jenny thought ruefully. She lifted a blue crimplene frock from somewhere near the bottom of her case, shook it out, and quietly thanked Providence under her breath that it showed no creases.

Nicole, now in front of the mirror, was putting the finishing touches to her make-up. She did not have to turn round to take note that Jenny was about to slip her dress over her head.

"That will do quite nicely," she said between closing her lipstick and flicking the powder brush once more along the line of her cheekbone.

"Very simple," Jenny admitted briefly. She patted her dress down to make doubly sure there was no creasing.

"Well, you're a very simple girl, aren't you, Jenny?" Nicole was at work with a tiny black brush, adding mascara to her lower eyelashes.

"Is 'simple' a word meaning 'country girl?' " Jenny asked.

"Well, yes—I suppose. Perhaps I really mean unsophisticated. Do you work at it? Hard?

Jenny's head emerged through the neckline of her dress. She stared at Nicole in surprise.

"Work at it? I don't understand."

"There you are. Exactly what I said." Nicole used an eyebrow brush, put it on the tray, then stood back and ran the palms of her hands down her hipline. She was appraising herself in the mirror.

"Unsophisticated!" she repeated. "Do remember that as a piece of advice. It is not a mere statement. You may know the southwest bush, dear girl. But you know absolutely nothing about the north and east. Don't attempt to do anything, however seemingly unimportant, without first asking me. And that goes for handling Drew, too. We—that is, Drew and I—understand one another. You will see that as we go along. Meantime—" She paused.

"Yes? Meantime?" Jenny was wondering how Nicole had arranged her short, slightly curled hair to set so neatly to the shape of her head. And in so short a time. Nicole might have stepped out of a bandbox.

She turned round now, and literally looked Jenny over.

"That's quite a nice dress," she said, nodding her head. "You'll pass. This is our first evening together as a whole party, Jenny. It's an opportunity to get to know one another. You do see that? You and Geoff are friends, of course." She paused, lifting her eyebrows in an enquiring way. "More than friends, perhaps?"

Jenny was taken aback.

"Old friends," she said with a small smile. "Born in the same town, and brought up in the same group. We played hoopla together as kittens. But about being 'something more?' You ask Geoff. He'll probably tell you I have other friends of staggering interest back in Yaraandoo. That is, besides himself. In fact, being able to look at me objectively, as it were, he'll know more about me than I know myself."

Nicole's manner was suddenly placating.

"All to the good!" she said. "Do you want the mirror? Actually you'll pass with just a dash of lipstick. The young-girl look does rather suit you, I must admit. But don't get under Drew's feet with small-town talk, will you? He has much on his mind. By the same token, so have I. You don't mind my giving you advice?"

They were looking at one another.

"Not in the least." Jenny smiled as warmly as she could. "I'll be glad of it. I won't make mistakes that way, will I? Well, not many, anyway!"

Nicole led the way from Number eleven. Outside Number twelve she gave a rat-a-tat code signal on the door.

Her hand was still in the air when the door opened, almost as if the signal had been eagerly awaited.

But it was only Geoff. Jenny could almost see the adroit angle of Nicole's head alter direction.

"Oh, it's you, Geoff, is it?" Nicole looked down as if the one-inch doorstep needed to be seen in order safely to be navigated. This thought made Jenny want to laugh, but at the same time she was a little ashamed of herself. The expressionless look on Geoff's face carried its own message, even though he was steadily and politely looking at Nicole.

"Enter, madam," he said with mock bow. "His High and Mightiness is waiting at the Battling Bar."

Nicole swept past Geoff without a word. He winked at Jenny, and this said a bookful.

"There you are, Drew." Nicole's voice floated outwards. "Sorry to keep you waiting, but Jenny was the littlest bit longer dressing than necessary." From the depths of the inside of Number twelve, her voice came lower. It was faintly suggestive of intimacy now.

Jenny, still on the doorstep, was trying another exchange of glances with Geoff, this time to tell him not to be silly. In fact, over the low voices inside, Geoff was also communicating advice to Jenny. "That's how

Nicole likes it. Always to be made to feel as important as she really is."

"I bet you say things behind my back, too," Jenny whispered as she in turn walked past him.

"But always!" Geoff agreed.

Once she was right inside, Jenny wished she hadn't been in such a hurry to follow Nicole. Drew, because of his tallness, had to bend over the low corner table on which were set the glasses, an ice bowl, and two bottles. He was in the act of using a small pair of tongs to lift ice from the bowl into one of the glasses. Nicole had put one hand on his shoulder in an intimate way. For the fraction of a minute Jenny felt a twinge of embarrassment; maybe she had come into the room too quickly.

Drew, partly turning, looked up and saw her. At the same time Nicole's hand slid from his shoulder back to her side. Jenny was looking at the unexpected charm of Drew's half smile as he welcomed her in.

"Oh, there you are, Jenny," he said. "Just in time. Is it to be a shandy? Or a man's drink? Namely, beer?"

"A shandy, please." She smiled back at him. For a split moment she was glowing inside herself; and like the soft lace of a long slip, something in her was showing. Nicole froze. Geoff, closing the door behind him, also noticed it.

Wow! Jenny girl! he thought. Don't go round looking like that or you'll have a scratch-cat on your back. Drew's booked for keeps by another lady, and she's right in front of you. Watching.

Drinks and their accompaniment of small talk did not last long. Roadhouses on the way to distant places were not like hotels. Staff was hard to come by, so visitors invariably obliged by being punctual for meals, as well as doing as much as they could for themselves.

As they all presently walked across the square to the dining room, Jenny felt herself aglow again. A watchful imp inside her was whispering, "Careful, Jenny! Something is going to your head. And it's not that very weak shandy."

But she wasn't willing to listen to small voices. Suddenly she felt that it was this very minute that her great adventure was really beginning. All that had gone before since she and Geoff had left the forest country had been only preliminary. Somehow, something climactic had happened in her life when she had walked through the doorway of Number twelve and Drew had smiled at her just that way. She had smiled back that way, too. She had felt young, gay, adventurous. And as her lips had taken the first sip of the shandy, her eyes had met Drew's eyes again. That was when she guessed she had, metaphorically speaking, thrown her hat in the air.

Now she was free.

She would not ask herself of what she was free. She would think about that another time. Now was for now, and she had to hold it to her as a child might try to hold a soap bubble, and keep it whole.

At the table they talked lightly of this and that, but mostly of bush food and bush cooking as found in roadhouses and stopovers along the cross-continental tracks and roads.

"Ah, but Jenny is a cook," said Nicole. "That's her job, of course, isn't it?" She smiled carefully across the table. "Be careful of the salt when we get right Outback, Jenny," she advised. "We need more of it in the high temperature zone, that's true; but it's wiser to take it in tablets than to put too much in the soup."

Geoff's eyes would have said, "I told you so!" But Jenny was not looking at them. Instead, it was Geoff himself who was now caught in Nicole's net. She turned to him and gave one of her best smiles. A really dazzling one.

"Perhaps her mind is on other things when in the kitchen. Do tell us, Geoff. What was it someone said about her VIP boy friend in that country town? What was it called? Oh, yes. Yaraandoo! Is he a farmer? Of course, all farmers' wives have to be good cooks, don't they? I hope Jenny won't be just *practising* on us."

"Boy friend?" asked Geoff, pretending vagueness. "Did she tell you I'd talk about him? Well, well!" He shook his head knowingly. "Wanted you to know about her gallery of admirers, hey?"

"Like you, for instance?" Jenny asked, sceptically. She was angry deep inside, but had to hide it. Who had talked? Geoff or Paul Collett?

"Me? What? *Me?*" Geoff asked, looking askance. "Don't stand a chance against John-o, do I? Yes, that's who he is, Nicole, if you must know." Geoff put on a dejected air. "John Downing, no less," he added. "Ever heard of him? I bet you haven't. But he's all for Jenny. Even has the blessings of her family, and at least two-thirds of the meagre population of Yaraandoo."

Jenny did not see Nicole's quick glance at Drew, nor the studied look of no interest on Drew's face as he crumbled a bread roll on his plate.

"Are you formally engaged yet?"' Nicole asked, sounding quite kind. Her eyes strayed to Jenny's left hand.

"No. No." Jenny was troubled now. She owed John loyalty. He had been her friend—asked or not. She was almost fond of him, the way one was fond of an ordinary family member, although not in any rainbow-coloured way.

"Not yet?" Nicole asked, her eyebrows raised. "Oh, well! That's life, isn't it? It's always the girl who has to do the waiting. Even in this free-and-easy day. Take my advice, Jenny, and next time you see him, *you* do the asking. You might get a pleasant surprise."

"And find herself falling into open arms," Geoff added lugubriously. For some reason he sounded angry.

Jenny's natural spirit came to her aid.

"Not till I've forgiven him for selling Redcoat," she began.

"Redcoat?" asked Nicole.

"That was her favourite horse," Geoff explained. "John didn't approve of her racing over the hill tops and—"

"I think," Drew Carey interrupted quite firmly, "we've had enough of discussing personalities."

Had he caught something shining behind Jenny's

eyes at the mention of Redcoat? Did he think it was because of John? She could have told him about Redcoat—but not here or now. She owed John that much. Still, it wasn't the first time Redcoat's name had brought that stinging feeling to Jenny's eyes.

"But of course," Nicole was saying, with the sort of gaiety that one assumes in order to put someone else into a cheerful state of mind. "Let's talk about opals, shall we? They're so very bright and colourful, and that's just what we need at the moment. Colour and cheer."

"What about black opals?" asked Geoff, rallying to the cause. "More precious and less colourful. That's our business out here in the wilds, isn't it? Or isn't it?"

"Black opals *can* be rich in colour, if you look deep into them," Drew said. "They're more valuable only because they are more rare. Precious opals—as such—are rarer still, and rank with diamonds, emeralds, and sapphires as *gems.*"

"To be distinguished from *gemstones,*" Nicole finished with an authoritative flourish. She was looking at Jenny with an extra-friendly smile—explaining to a child, as it were. Drew put his hand into his pocket and drew out a small, round tobacco tin. With infinite care he eased off the lid.

One by one he set out a number of different-coloured small stones in a circle on the white tablecloth.

He pushed his plate aside and touched the one nearest to him.

"This lot are in their natural state except that they've been tumble-polished," he said. "That's why they shine. This particular one, with the lovely mauve shades, is alexandrite. The one opposite it has been cut with a round top, so it's a cabochon. You can see how much brighter it is. Richer in colour, too. It is the same stone, but treated in a more sophisticated way. This green one is tourmaline—as lovely as emerald but not so hard. It's nothing like so rare, either; so it's a gemstone and not a gem." He looked up at Jenny and his eyes met hers, holding them. His voice was somehow compelling—as if he were talking to her alone.

He's trying to take my mind off Redcoat, she thought. He's not an Ogre Boss at all. He's wise. He sees into one.

"So if you ever want a green stone for your engagement ring, Jenny," Nicole put in, "be sure it's an emerald and not a tourmaline. An emerald is much, much more valuable."

"But this is just as lovely," Jenny said of the tourmaline. "Darker, but sort of mysterious." She looked lovingly at the gem and, thinking of it, missed the implication of her own answer.

Geoff exchanged a glance with Nicole.

"I'd say someone is getting off lightly," he whispered.

Drew heard him, and had Jenny been looking at Drew then, she would have seen that the "Boss Fella" in him could really rear his head, given the cause.

"This green and white stone is beryl," Drew went on, as if nothing had happened. "It comes in different colours, but I have only this specimen with me."

"And that beautiful mauve one?" Jenny asked.

"Amethyst." Drew looked up and smiled at her. He liked her nearly childlike wonder at his small display. "That's one you should have guessed, you know, Jenny. It has given its name to its color."

"Yes, of course." Jenny admitted her ignorance without shame. The lovely stones were giving her such delight!

Drew's fingers travelled round the circle, naming each stone as his finger stopped. "Spinel—that's bluer than blue sapphire. Garnet—very like a ruby in colour. Topaz—rock crystal. Moonstone—" He paused and looked up at Jenny again.

"I'm sorry," she said. "You're right. I'm not taking in which names belong to what. I think it might—"

"—take you some time to remember them all? Stop worrying—as of now. You don't have to remember them. You'll discover them for yourself as you go along. And each has certain distinctions. That's called lithology. Have you heard that word before?"

Jenny shook her head, her eyes still held by Drew's eyes. He was a different man. He loved his gemstones and had found a willing listener.

"She doesn't have to know this—what do you call it?—lithology, does she?" Geoff asked, suddenly out of character and all protection for Jenny. "She's the cook, bottle-washer, and rouseabout, isn't she?" He turned to Nicole, slightly aggressive. "What about you? Are you knowledgeable about all these long words ending in 'ol-ogy?' "

"I'm knowledgeable about the physical properties that determine the character of rocks. And that's one way of saying 'lithology,' " Nicole said coldly. "You needn't raise your eyebrows, Geoff. I'm not a geologist nor even Drew's kind of professional gem collector. But I keep my eyes open and my ears tuned. And I remember. Have you got the message?"

"It's as simple as that?"

"As simple as that. A good memory. Unless—" She looked at Jenny again. Jenny, for her part, felt in her bones that Nicole was about to end her sentence with the words, *unless you're a simpleton.* The other, how-ever, was only looking her over. The rest of the sen-tence did not come."

Drew scooped the gems together into a neat pile and tumbled them back into the box.

"That's enough for tonight," he said briefly. He glanced from Geoff to Jenny. "I was testing to see if there was a spark of interest. As you said, Geoff, Jenny's work will be of another kind, but you never can tell. She might be the one to stumble on a strike."

"Good for Jenny!" Geoff didn't exactly grumble. He was feeling a little respect for Drew's authority. But he gave Jenny's foot a slight push with his boot. In effect, he was saying "Look out, luv. This beast when at-tacked defends itself. And could come out the winner."

Jenny remained silent, leaving Geoff and Drew to outstare one another.

Suddenly she felt lighter than air. Dear old Geoff. In his own way he was defending her. She felt a little catch in her heart. The expression in his eyes touched her in the place where she was most vulnerable.

She came back to earth when she realized that Drew's attention was again on her.

"End of the preliminary lesson," he said briefly. "Each day—when we're able—we'll take it a little further and discuss colour, lustre, streak, hardness, and crystal structures as a means of identification." His voice was more friendly, in a subtle kind of way. He must have been watching her reaction to the stones when he had shown them earlier. "I think you'll like it, Jenny," he said quietly. "You don't cook or wash bottles all day on a safari, you know. There *are* hours in between."

"And I just might be the one to kick over an opal pad?" she asked brightly.

"You just might," he said. "If such a thing were kickable over." He pocketed his box and pushed back his chair.

"An opal pad," Nicole explained considerately, "is a whole *area* of metamorphic rocks with the right specialized characteristics for opals. Those characteristics are—"

Drew was already standing and Geoff made a scraping noise with his chair legs as he followed suit.

"That will be our next lesson, Nicole," Drew interrupted quietly. He turned to Jenny. "I hope you don't read in bed too late. It's an early start tomorrow. Five-thirty in the kitchen. That's where the staff serves a light breakfast for the early starters. We help ourselves, in the kitchen, in these Outback areas."

They were all standing now.

"I shan't read at all tonight," Jenny said. "I'm tired already. Will it be all right if I'm first in the kitchen in the morning? After all, I *am* the cook, aren't I?"

Drew raised his eyebrows as if surprised.

"Good girl!" he said. "A boiling kettle is the best beginning for an early start. Don't get under the cook's feet, and she'll welcome you if you give a hand."

"And she *can* boil a kettle," Geoff added, indicating Jenny. "I've seen her do it at the local gymkhanas in—"

"In Yaraandoo," Drew finished for him. "Yes. Quite. If you would kindly see Jenny to her door, Geoff?" Nicole and I have some matters to talk over."

"Matters!" Geoff muttered as they went off. "That's what he calls a spot of good-night love-making, I suppose. I bet you'll be way off in dreamland by the time Nicole comes to bed."

6

Geoff was right. Jenny was so tired by the time she reached her room that she didn't have even the energy to wonder any longer whether she did, or did not, really like Drew Carey. She was no sooner in bed than her eyelids drooped over her eyes. She was almost instantly asleep, and didn't know what hour Nicole came in.

In the false dawn of early morning her tiny alarm clock tinkled lightly. Wow! How cold can it get in these parts at this hour, she thought as she scrambled out of bed. She made for the shower alcove at top speed and turned on the hot water to warm as much as to wash herself.

Coming back into the room, wrapped in a towel, she turned the thermostat half way to 'Hot' before she shook Nicole gently by the shoulder.

"Up, Up," she said gently. "Breakfast in half an hour!"

"Oh! For goodness sake! I've only had that much time for sleep." Nicole was not pleased. "At least it seems that way."

Seems? Jenny wondered. Or *was?* Somehow the idea was just a little depressing.

She began getting ready at top speed. She would show Big Boss Fella who was the efficient body today. Herself! In the kitchen she would come into her own and demonstrate that though she might not know what certain types of rocks were, she did know that if you give a man a good breakfast, you'll have him on your

44

side for the day. She wasn't a farmer's daughter for nothing.

Her clothes went on in record time. Her handkerchief was stuffed in the pocket of her safari jacket, her money-purse buttoned into the top outside pocket, and her small comb and lipstick crammed into the lower left-hand one.

Oh so pocket-full of wonders are these safari outfits! she thought. Then she looked under her pillow and in the two drawers, in case she had left something behind. As a last-minute reversal of general procedures she plaited her long hair in a tail and fixed that same tail into a good-behaviour pattern by binding it with a rubber band.

She took one last glimpse at herself in the mirror before slapping on her hat at a truly professional, Outback angle.

"You'll do!" she addressed herself. "Now here goes for the kitchen! My first day!"

As she went through the door she was aware that Nicole's eyes were very wide open, and looking at her.

"Well!" Jenny murmured, out of hearing. "If Mr. Drew Carey kept you up all those hours, let him come himself to wake you up properly and, no doubt, in a loverly way."

She wondered if she was being mean. She very nearly went back, except that, after all, Nicole's eyes *had* been open! She herself could be an embarrassment if Drew did indeed come to wake his sleeping beauty. She was already awake anyhow. And—maybe—waiting?

The back entrance of the roadhouse was still locked up. For a moment Jenny was nonplussed.

As she turned round, she saw a man standing in the pale, early-morning light under the night shadow of a bank of trees over to the right. He stood quite still, his hands deep in the pockets of his jeans. He wore a white, round-brimmed cotton hat with the narrow brim turned down all round. He was so still, and the trees

were so still. It was as if the whole world was half-
asleep and herself and this strange shadow of a man
were the only people in the entire Outback.

He was watching her. Yet he did not move or speak.
His eyes were only shadows in his face; yet strangely
she thought, or imagined, that she could see his eyes
and that they were bright and hard in their dark sock-
ets and that they were taking her in—every tiny part,
every inch of her.

Jenny shook herself. Well, there were baddies as well
as goodies in the Outback. Like all over the world. She
turned to find her way back to the front entrance and
was tempted to run. But some inner voice told her to
walk normally—as if nothing were wrong. And this she
did. It was the first time in her life she had walked on
past someone without nodding and saying, "Good
morning!"

Funny, she thought as she put her overnight bag just
inside the big glass door, her cotton hat now stuffed in
the handle for safekeeping. He quite gave me a chill!
What was he doing there all alone in the shadows, not
speaking? Everyone in the country speaks.

But then I didn't speak myself, did I? she told herself.

Vaguely she felt ashamed that she had passed him
by, and had not—at the very least—smiled. But there
had been something about the man and the shadows
around him. He had the wrong hat on for the Outback,
too. White, and just a tiny narrow brim that flopped
down almost over his eyes. And he wore jeans.
Whereas she knew that everyone Outback wore jungle
hats or wide-brimmed khaki stetsons, and khaki shorts.

He was someone from somewhere else. He didn't belong. Perhaps that was what was odd about him. Well,
of course, he couldn't be a potential bushranger now,
could he? Jenny almost laughed at herself.

Once inside the main entrance Jenny saw the narrow
side door that had to lead to the kitchen. She forgot
about strange men wearing wrong clothes for the Outback. She turned the door handle and walked through,

shutting the door behind her. She had the strangest feeling of relief as she went down the narrow passage, through another short entry, and into the bright, already inhabited kitchen.

The fire glowed and crackled in the stove (which had an enormous range behind it), and there were people there. It was almost a crowd, for a kitchen.

Here was another safari party; she knew that. And by the look of things they, too, were to breakfast in what was called the "back diner." It was a room with many tables just through an enormous archway from the main kitchen. These people, like Drew and Drew's party, were the extra-early risers who wanted sustenance before the main dining room was open.

The cook, a large stout woman with a jolly face, gave Jenny a bustling look, and went on with the business of frying bacon and grilling steak at the same time.

"Please, may I help?" Jenny said at once, speaking to a broad back.

"With all that mob stampeding in my kitchen before six?" the cook said, not turning. "Not on your life! 'What's mine's mine,' I said to the Boss last night. 'An' what you've got you have to look after,' I added. 'No fat spilled on the floor, and no cracked plates. Not to mention missing teaspoons.' That's what I said, and I meant it!"

"I have to please my boss, too," Jenny said.

The cook turned round and looked her up and down.

"You from the country? Or you a towny?" she asked.

"From the southwest country. From a farm," Jenny said hopefully.

"Then that's all right with me. Here, you take the bacon and I'll fix the steak. Then you can set the window end of the big table in the alcove for your crowd. The other lot are just on finished. Which lot are you?" The cook was no longer looking at Jenny but was already turning the steak over on the open-fire section of the stove.

"The Drew Carey safari."

The cook stopped work. She now had a piece of steak held in mid-air as she turned her head.

"Oh, him!" she said. "Well, if you're with his lot you're okay working in my kitchen. And you can get along as fast as you like. A real gentleman is Drew Carey. Comes this way often, but mostly just himself with a rouseabout. This time it's a safari, is it? Well, good luck to him! He's a man I take to, and the boss says so, too. Always remembers to say, 'Goodbye. I'll see you another time. Thank you.' Never misses. Never insults by passing a tip, either. Just sends me a card and one of them gemstones of his. I'm getting a real collection—if I only knew what they was called!"

She prattled on nonstop, but Jenny felt her heart warmed.

So he is genuine, she thought. He might play human beings as if they were pieces in a game of chess, but he plays fair.

While grilling strips of bacon she reflected on all that had happened so far, including the strange, shadowy man outside.

But she thought mostly of Drew.

Those eyes that were almost friendly one moment and then developed a compelling, "Ten-shun!" look in them the next!

Or did she imagine it all? She wished she could stop thinking about him. Why did a boss—just because he was a "boss"—have an extra lustre about him?

"You can set the places for Drew and his mob at the end of the table by the window," the cook told Jenny again when the grilling was done and the bacon resting on a plate in the oven. "That's pride of place; so you'd better set it up quick before the lot from Ukabarra Station come in."

A large tray of cutlery rested on one of the benches against the wall, and Jenny hurried to obey. Being one of "Drew's mob," she had a vested interest in seeing her boss had the best place.

She had barely put the knives and forks out when

the door was pushed open and a station owner walked in. He was tall and spare. His face, hands, and bared arms were grilled brown by constant exposure to the sun. And he wore the right uniform for the Outback: khaki shorts and shirt. The hat in his hand was a broad-brimmed, dusty stetson.

"Morning, Mrs. Burton," he said with a nod. He walked with a stride that was magically brusque in manner but quiet in sound towards the top end of the table. There were pegs on the wall behind him, and there he hung his hat.

"Morning, miss, and who are you setting for?" he asked sharply as he glanced at Jenny.

"Drew Carey's party," she said. She didn't quite look up, but she was sure the station owner and Mrs. Burton—if that really was the cook's name—exchanged a glance. Jenny sighed. Probably in these Outbackish parts one did not speak of "a party." It gave her away as a "down-south." It was the same thing as showing herself to be a stranger. "Mob" apparently was the correct appellation hereabouts for any group exceeding one in number. But she didn't have time to correct her own use of English, for the door opened again with a wide sweep. Drew came in.

"Hi there, Carey!" the station owner greeted him quite cheerfully. "So you made it after all? I was about to leave and let *you* come to *me*."

"Then I've caught you just in time!"

The two men met in the middle of the floor and shook hands in a way that made Jenny wince. Those hands must be made of iron, she thought.

"That's right," Drew went on. "I have the document with me. Oh, you've met Jenny—" His hand went to his forehead. "Must have had a late night," he said, with an apologetic grin. "I can't remember your other name, Jenny."

"Haseltine," she said. Was she so unimportant that Drew couldn't even remember her surname? "Jenny Haseltine," she repeated. She offered the station owner a small smile, then bent her head over the place-setting business again.

"One of my rouseabouts," Drew explained. "We have girls for that sort of work in this day and age. She can cook, too. Jenny, this is Nat Barrett from Ukabarra Station. We might be trespassing on his property late in the safari; so you'd better get acquainted now."

Jenny offered a small smile. She said, "How do you do?" instead of "Hi, there!" or whatever one was supposed to say in these outlands. She'd used the formal greeting on purpose.

This Nat man exchanged a glance with Drew similar to the one he had shared with Mrs. Burton earlier; but Jenny's heart lifted because Drew also gave her a smile. It was that shining one. She'd only seen it once before—when they'd first met. He knew she had said that "How do you do?" on purpose, and he had thought it clever, or something like it. He even appreciated it. She hadn't let the big, important station man look down at her because she was "just a rouseabout."

One up to me! she thought, busy setting the plates around. How about that game of chess now? I think I'll keep a tally of points for and against. It's easier than thinking of pawns, kings, and queens. Castles, too, since Mr. Nat Barrett owned a station, and everyone knew that station owners were kings in their castles once they went striding over their million-acre leaseholds.

Drew and Nat Barrett moved to a side table by the far wall. Drew pulled a brown wallet from his hip pocket as he dropped his voice and went on talking quietly.

The door swung open again and Nicole came in.

Jenny drew in a breath, for Nicole really did look an early-morning beauty! She was dressed in a fresh tan-coloured safari jacket with a short skirt. She didn't look one bit like "late hours." But then make-up—faint, tan, and beautifully applied—helped her there. Jenny acknowledged that. She did not want to feel mean about it; but she *was* naturally and admiringly envious. Nicole's figure was so slim, and the "tailored look" suited her. She had beautiful legs and ankles, too. They were worth showing. Her hair had been carefully brushed and her perfect white teeth shone in her lively, tanned face. Jenny tried to banish her jealousy. One had to be a good sport about these things, she knew. When she had time she would count her own blessings!

"Hallo, Nat, old dear!" Nicole said, not bothering with anyone else in the kitchen. She addressed herself exclusively to the two men by the side table. "You've really come to the party, I see!"

To Jenny's amazement Nicole seemed to be just a little bit affected as she greeted the station owner. And he seemed to behave a trifle differently, too.

"If you mean putting my name to this so-and-so proposition you and Drew have dreamed up," he said with a grin, "well, I suppose you can call it 'a party' on *your* side of the fence. But how we'll manage as a threesome I'm not so sure! We'd better make it worthwhile—or I'll have my stable-mate on my back."

He meant his wife, Jenny supposed. Yet there had been some extra meaning in his words as he and Nicole exchanged a kind of a special message one to the other.

"By the way, where *is* your family?" Drew asked as he took a quarto-sized document from his leather folder-wallet and spread it on the side table.

"They're still in bed. And with Mrs. Burton's good will they'll have a tray sent over. The children possibly will eat later. I was up early as I had a hunch when we pulled in that you might make it last night. The parking space is littered with Land Rovers and Land Cruisers. Not all yours, I hope?"

"No. There's another safari party in. Still abed possibly. Tourists, I imagine."

Jenny stopped listening to the conversation as she crossed the kitchen back to the stove.

"If they're about to talk business," she whispered to Mrs. Burton, "do you think the bacon might dry to a crackle, and I'd better do some more?"

"No, leave it be," Mrs. Burton said bluntly. "They're

putting their names to that piece of paper. You watch and they'll call me over to witness their signatures. Yours too, more'n likely. The papers I've signed as witness round these parts these last two years! You wouldn't read about it! Every Tom, Dick, and Harry pegging a mining lease. Not to mention the regular prospectors—"

"Why is that?" Jenny was puzzled.

"The nickel boom and that new copper strike. And—would you believe it? *Gold's* on the comeback. Gone up in price, they say. There's even some of the gold mines in the ghost towns northeast they're thinking of opening up again!"

Jenny was too discreet to say, "It's not nickel or gold *we're* interested in. It's opal." But she nodded her head sagely at the words "ghost towns." She'd heard all about them, read all about them. Now she was hoping to see them.

"Yes, ghost towns!" was all she said while she watched Mrs. Burton slap dabs of butter on the steaks and return the dish to the oven.

Behind her Drew, Nicole, and Nat Barrett were saying very little. They passed a fountain pen from one to the other and each signed that sacred document, whatever it was.

"Mrs. Burton, can you spare a moment?" It was Drew's voice.

"Told you so, didn't I?" whispered Mrs. Burton. "Your turn next."

Jenny felt positively uneasy. She couldn't help being a *little* curious about that document, mainly because both Nicole and Drew seemed to have some business concern in it. Geoff had said Nicole had "money"— meaning a lot of it. Did that mean she was financing Drew? Jenny found herself hoping not. In her heart she *wanted* Drew to be the Big Boss Fella—someone skillful and able in his own right and not someone tied irrevocably to Nicole. That is, and she had to be fair, unless he really was in love with Nicole.

Oh dear! And I hardly know them! she thought.

Why don't I mind my own business?

The kitchen door swung open again and Geoff—barely hiding a yawn—came in. Jenny's world was suddenly brighter. Dear Geoff, she thought—for no particular reason, except that he was one of her own kind. She felt sort of safer when Geoff was near. Which was ridiculous, of course.

"'Morning everyone!" he said. "Sorry I'm last but someone has to be that, eh? Ladies first through doors, anyway."

"'Morning, Geoff." Drew half turned round. "You're just in time. We want your signature over here. This is Nat Barrett of Ukabarra, Geoff. Nat, this is Geoff Hallam, my strong-arm man for the duration."

Jenny was relieved. She didn't know if, being under twenty-one, she could witness signatures anyway. And for some odd reason she did not now want to see that piece of paper. She didn't want to have anything to do with it. She went on fussing with the toast and did not once turn round. She was just the rouseabout, wasn't she?

7

They were on their way again. And it was a lovely day!

The early morning wind had dropped and the sun took the chill from the air. The salmon gums stretching their long slim arms upwards to make leafy rooftops were, as ever, rooted in their still and statuesque silence. The red gravel road and the clay earth between the trees shone in a subdued way. The world was full of colour. Jenny forgot, for the present, the strange man under the trees back at the motel. Her spirits were high again. "I'm on my way," she all but sang under her breath.

"What goes with you?" Geoff asked. He paused in his whistling through his teeth and glanced sideways at Jenny. "Head up in the air. Eyes sparkling. You know what? I'm learning something. You're downright pretty when you're in this mood. And no one's been kissing you this last forty-eight hours, I'll swear to that!"

"You've been keeping guard, have you?" Jenny asked, without turning her head.

"Well, while Nicole and Drew were busy last night I took myself a walk in the bush—leastways along the gravel track leading off somewhere into the trees. So I'd have seen anyone about, wouldn't I? As a matter of fact, all I did see was your night-light on. I nearly called you out myself. Would you have come?" Geoff had a curious note in his voice as he asked that question.

"I wish you had done just that," Jenny said. "Last thing when I did turn in was to look through my window. It was lovely out there in the bush last night. The moon was up; the stars were bright. It was absolutely brilliant outside. And the trees made patterns on the ground." She paused. Her voice dropped a little. "What do you mean by 'Nicole and Drew were *busy?*' Do you think—?"

"I don't *think* a thing about what they're at. I just suspect. And my suspicion is that it's business. Business first, anyway. Guess they were deciding whether we'd go up north through the ghost towns to that old goldfields patch forgotten half a century ago or make for good old Kalgoorlie and the Golden Mile and on to Karonie where they—meaning some other people— have just made a strike of the real stuff. Precious opal, I mean—not gold. Problem is, how to get on that sheep station without permission in advance. Every Tom, Dick, and Harry in the game will be battling to get over the stock-catchers grid in battalion formation. Say, Jenny? From your first lesson in lithology last night you registered the difference between precious opal and plain opal?"

"Barely. Except that one's more precious and so must be more valuable than the other."

"*Scarcer,* and more beautiful. Don't forget the imperatives, sweetheart."

"Well—" Jenny was watching Geoff's right hand fish for a cigarette from the packet in his top pocket. "Well, I suppose those are the imperatives for Nicole and Drew," she said. "I mean business first, and all that. But other than that—I mean, do you think—?"

Geoff's eyes slid round to see Jenny's face. Her startling blue eyes were looking at him in a very serious way.

"You mean are they making out together? How the heck do I know? I don't keep watch on Drew. If they're in love, they're in love. And that's it. So what of it?"

"I don't know. We're such a small party, aren't we? It's so easy to get sort of interested in the other people. Not in any unkind way." Jenny glanced out of her side window, then added wistfully, " 'All mankind loves a lover,' I guess. Who said that? Or did I make it up? It sounds right, anyway."

"You made it up," Geoff said flatly. His speed was fast, and he saw a break in the road coming up.

"Hang on!" he exclaimed. "Wow, that was a pot hole and a half, wasn't it? Bump your head or anything?"

"No," Jenny said. "I saw it coming before you did. You didn't slow down in time. You should watch for shadows in the road, Geoff. I mean unusual shadows. It generally means a depression and—"

—on a gravel track a depression means a pot hole! Okay, okay! Don't turn into a lecturer, Jenny. I might tip you out the next hole I hit."

"When do we get on to the bitumen again?" Jenny asked coldly. "Drew did say Coolgardie, next stop, didn't he?"

"He did. And is what you're doing right now, sweetheart, changing the subject? Okay. Subject's changed. Wow! Watch it."

The Rover jerked up, then down, then up again. In the front seats they rattled like two peas in a pod.

"Shall I take over?" Jenny asked serenely.

"And pay me a dollar for every pot hole *you* hit? No, infant. I'll spare you going bankrupt on this run."

The Rover wound its way between trees and over miniature claypans, through tougher bush, and at last on to the bitumen.

"Speed limit's sixty-five miles an hour," sang Geoff in a make-believe falsetto. "Watch me make Coolgardie in time for snacks—at nothing less than eighty mph."

Jenny grasped the door handle firmly, and said nothing. She knew everyone drove at eighty on the long stretches; so there was no point in her protesting.

On the outskirts of the ancient gold-fields ghost town Drew, who'd gone ahead, flagged them down.

"I'm going out to see old Pete the Prospector's mullock heap," he said through the window to Geoff. "But I'll need your Rover to get through that bush track to

Pete's shack. Would you mind taking over in mine, Geoff, and going on to the pub? The corner one on the opposite side from the old Government Buildings. It's about the only place still going—and temporarily at that. You can't miss the old buildings. They're a monument to past gold-boom days."

"Sure," Geoff said, pulling the hand brake tighter. "What about you, Jenny? Coming with me, or going with him?"

What a choice!

Jenny longed to "go with him." If she'd been Caroline, the first girl chosen for this safari, she would have invited herself forthwith. But she was only Jenny, a runaway girl. So she was the petitioning one, not the decision-maker. She was here to do as she was told.

Drew had turned away and was making hand signals to Nicole.

Geoff opened the door and was easing himself out. "How about Jenny, Drew?" he asked again. "Maybe she's never seen an old prospector on the job. There wouldn't be a dozen of the oldtimers left now."

Jenny's blue-blue eyes were looking at Drew with a kind of hope in them that she could not hide.

"Well, yes—" Drew said. Jenny feared this was almost grudging. "That is," he went on, "if she can stand the pot holes. It's a bad track."

"She'll see them coming ahead of time," Geoff said. "She darn-all does before *I* can. And praise the pebbles, she doesn't talk too much." He had opened the door and jumped to the ground.

Jenny was grateful for Geoff's help, so she let that last part of his remarks go unchallenged. He had asked, in his own way, for Drew to take her. She could have kissed him. Instead, she watched Drew's face to see his reaction. Her eyes all but pleaded, but she had no idea of that.

"Okay," Drew said quietly. "You'd like to come, I take it, Jenny?"

"Yes. I'd like it very much. That is—"

"If I agree? It seems to me that it's Geoff who's calling the order of the day." Even as he spoke he was swinging himself up on to the driver's seat.

"We could take it in turns to drive," she said, as she climbed in on the other side. She had to impress him with the idea that she was adult and not only, as he already knew, could drive a Land Rover, but could also see pot holes in advance while she was driving. She thought it was important that she start off by demonstrating her usefulness.

He said nothing. He lifted his hand to Geoff in the kind of Outback salute that said "Hallo" or "Goodbye" according to the moment.

Drew started up and took off at quite a pace.

Oh, what a wonderful day! Jenny thought. She nearly hummed the tune.

They were on the edge of the Outback now. Kalgoorlie, the gold-mining centre twenty miles on from Coolgardie, was coming up. After that, there'd be one or two semi-desert sheep stations. Then the *real* Outback.

Her heart lifted. She was really going places now. And with Drew! Perhaps she might get to know him better!

She glanced round at him. He had swerved the vehicle in a half-circle to make off down the gravel clay no-track that wound through the trees to the north.

"Well?" he said, keeping his eyes straight ahead. "What is it you were going to say, Jenny?"

It was almost as if he had been reading her thoughts without even looking at her.

"That it's a wonderful day," she said lamely.

He turned his head and glanced at her.

She wanted to whisper, "there's a pot hole coming up—" but didn't quite dare. He was a wonder driver, though. He'd seen that pot hole, too. Still looking at Jenny, he swerved the Rover ever so slightly so that the pot hole passed between the wheels and clean under them.

Jenny eased her hold on the door handle and breathed out.

"Phew!" she said, under her breath.

"Did you think I couldn't make it?" he asked. If there was a smile in his eyes, he didn't let her see it. Somewhere inside her something tender was touched. *Why did he turn out to be like this?* If he had stayed Big Boss Fella, it would have made it so much easier.

That way she could have wiped him from her mind—except, of course, for obeying his instructions. In spite of that smile, she could have managed very well to *not* think of him at all. He would have been no more to her than someone in authority, who gave out the orders, then went away and fixed his own affairs somewhere else.

"I wasn't thinking about the pot hole," she said, not quite truthfully. "Generally speaking, I've been thinking about the bush all day. The trees, the colour of their trunks—everything is so different from down south. That is, except—"

"Except what?"

"The eeriness. Even though it's broad daylight. It's sort of secretive. And indifferent. The bush, I mean. It's so *lonely!*"

Drew changed gears to lessen the speed as he took a right-angled turn. "But the *scent* of the bush. You haven't mentioned the scent, Jenny. Crush a gum leaf, or set a match to dry a bunch of leaves, and you're back home. Anywhere in the bush. North, south, east, or west."

"Yes. That's true." She felt easier now. "Even when I was up on a shopping spree in the city, the smell of gum leaves crackling in the burn-offs along King's Park verges made me feel homesick."

Drew changed into top gear again. They were really speeding. He did not answer her last remark; so she let the silence lie between them. This silence was comforting now. She had no idea why. It was as if the whole world was hers since she had fled the problems that had bothered her at home: John, Redcoat, her father who had so callously let John sell Redcoat.

She was Jenny-run-quickly on her way out of town.

"What are you thinking?" Drew asked. He was looking straight ahead.

"I was thinking of Yaraandoo,'" she said. "And why—" She broke off.

"Yes—why?" he said. "Why did you choose to come on this safari, for instance?"

"Doesn't everyone want to go away sometimes, even for a little while?"

"I imagine so. But I think *you* had some special reason."

"Are you a mind reader?"

"No. And I'm not an intruder in other people's affairs, either. I asked you because you said you were thinking of Yaraandoo. And your eyes had a troubled look in them."

"My eyes? But you're driving the Rover. And looking in front—well, you are now, anyway. Although you know this track already, don't you, Drew?"

"Yes. I could drive a Land Rover through it blind, except for kangaroos. You can't anticipate *them*. So I watch the track most of the time. But not every second of the time. I like to know how my driving companion is getting on. How are you getting on, Jenny?"

"Very well, thank you," she said firmly. "In spite of my eyes—" If it had been Geoff with his hands on that wheel, she would have finished with some fun talk, the way he and she always did. But she couldn't with Drew. She was too uncertain of him.

"Good. Then we'll settle for that," he said. "You feel very well in spite of your eyes. That's reassuring. Now we'll get on to another subject. It's the man I'm going to see. Round these parts they call him Pete the Prospector, and I've no idea if he has any other name. I've never asked. He collects gemstones for me. That is, if he comes across anything interesting. He's short on words, Jenny; so don't try to make conversation with him. Let him set the pace. Okay?"

"Yes. Okay."

"Good. By the way, I want to make his place before sundown. That will leave us time to get back to town for the last half of the dinner hour."

8

It was wild country, all right. Miles and miles and miles of it. North, south, east, west—it was a nothingness of low, blue-grass bush. Here and there were some straggly mulga trees. But only a few and always in clumps.

One could call it terrible, she thought, except for something mysterious about it—the fact that it goes on and on for ever, and is so flat.

The straight part of the track was no more than a narrow yellow line going way off to a horizon that they never reached.

"I think of the people coming out here in the days of the old gold rushes," she said, breaking the silence. "They must have had courage."

"You realize that?"

"Yes. My mother had an uncle who came out on a gold rush from Coolgardie." She paused. "He was only twenty. He was never heard of again."

"Those who died were buried by their mates wherever they dropped," Drew said. "Alhough there were some who wandered away, were lost, and probably died of thirst."

He sounded so factual. She thought, not for the first time, that perhaps he had a hard streak in him.

She nodded. She'd been told that before. But she couldn't bring herself to put it into words, as Drew had done.

"They came from all over the world," Drew went on, still in a firm tone. He had flicked the rear-vision mirror slightly so that it was angled towards her instead of to the rear window. The only thing she thought about him now was that he was so matter-of-fact. Did he have stone for a heart?

"They came from England, South Africa, and in one famous case from America. It was the world's greatest bonanza, that gold. And it's still here. Old dry-blowers like Pete the Prospector never stop looking."

"But what do they live on?" Jenny asked.

"Oh, they prospect around and find a bit here and there on the surface. They take out a miner's licence, and if the quartz is good and there're enough gold specks they peg a claim. They scratch around down the old shafts, round the mullock heaps. You'll see them—the mullock heaps—like ant hills around each of those old shafts. That reminds me, Jenny. Don't take a moonlight walk alone. That's an order. Those old shafts are dangerous. You could fall down one."

Fall down a shaft? They were just holes in the ground, weren't they?

"I'll be sure to remember," she said. She didn't intend to do any foolhardy things in a terrain which was new to her.

She kept her eyes straight ahead; yet she knew Drew had glanced down at her.

"Nicole knows every inch of these areas. I imagine she could plot a safe route in the pitch dark of a moonless night," he said. "If you want any advice, ask her. Right?"

Jenny nodded. She waited through some minutes of his silence, then decided to try a different tack.

"You said there was a very famous person who came here in the old gold-rush days?"

"Hoover from America," he said. "He managed the Sons of Gwalia mine further north. It was a very rich gold mine and has only lately become defunct. The town that grew up around that mine is now a ghost town. Quite celebrated by the National Trust and the Conservationists, of course. Quite possibly we will call in there sometime on this trip."

"Miners came in the gold-rush days from Cornwall

and Wales," Jenny said diffidently. "Was it just because he—I mean, this man called Hoover—came from America instead of England and Wales that he was important?"

Drew had the smallest of small smiles at the corners of his mouth as he replied.

"No. It wasn't where he came from that's put him in history books. It's what he went back to. He became the President of the United States of America. He was Mr. Herbert Hoover."

"Wow!" Jenny was properly impressed.

"If we detour that way you'll be able to see the house he lived in. The whole of the Sons of Gwalia area is full of interest in its own right."

"I would like that," Jenny said eagerly. "I'd like to see all the old mines."

"You'll see plenty of relics. Remember my advice, though. Some of them, the lesser ones where prospectors mined their own stone with hand and spade, are mere holes in the ground. You'll recognize most of those by the mullock heaps alongside. But don't go exploring too near if there's any rain. You could slip on the mullock. And don't go by yourself—especially at night. Right?"

"Yes. Right," Jenny said firmly. She looked up at him and once again caught the hint of a smile, in his eyes as well as at the corners of his mouth this time. She felt something like a wave of affection go out to him. He wasn't such an ogre, after all. He hadn't even minded her echoing his dynamic way of saying "right."

"Look over to your left," he said suddenly, sharply. Jenny turned her head.

"Oh!" she exclaimed. "Kangaroos! Dozens and dozens of them running through the bush. It's almost as if the bush is alive! There are so *many*!" A whole strip of the bush itself seemed to be moving. "They're the same colour. But where are they going? And why?"

"In search of food," Drew said flatly. "The kangaroos feed and the sheep die. That's ecology for you."

"You sound so—well—"

"Cynical? No, I'm not quite that. When you get a drought season such as there was last year, the race is to the swift. Kangaroos get to the grass first. And the sheep don't."

There was silence while Jenny digested this. If something, some animal had to die, did it matter which it was? A kangaroo or sheep?

"How dreadful!" was all she said.

"No one likes having to make a choice, Jenny," Drew said quietly, guessing at her thoughts. "But sometimes owners of sheep stations must make it."

"I know. They bring in the kangaroo shooters?"

"Exactly."

There was another silence.

"You have to come to terms with nature if you live hereabouts," Drew said finally. "There's no other way." He looked down at Jenny, and she looked up at him. His eyes were grave; yet somewhere deep in them was a message.

She looked away. Her heart was beating a little faster, but only because—in the world of her mind—she was in foreign country. She looked out of the window again. The kangaroos were gone now. There were only the grey, bush-slim sapling trees standing in utter silence above the carpet of red clay and low ground cover.

"So hungry looking, those trees," she said.

"So thirsty, too. Yet they survive," Drew said. "That's the mulga for you. It's easy to get lost here, by the way."

"Yes. Of course."

"No one who gets lost ever believes beforehand that it can happen to him. It's the sameness of the landscape. It deceives. The rule of the country is to stay in the shade of a mulga, scrappy though it is, and wait. Whenever you're not sure where you are, just *wait*. Have you got the message, Jenny?"

She nodded her head.

"But I'm not likely to be alone anywhere in the bush, am I?"

"No. But it's as well to know a little of bush lore, to hear about the land and all its vagaries. It's never the old hands who get lost. This can be a cruel country if you do not know it—especially cruel for the foolhardy. No riding a bush brumby over the hills and faraway out here."

"Geoff told you about Redcoat? My horse?"

"Yes. Was there any reason why he should not? When we bring a newcomer out here, we like to know as much as possible about that newcomer and his or her capacity to stand up to the country."

"I see."

"Geoff was already contracted on my staff. It was his duty to answer questions. They weren't so very personal, anyway."

"Did you ask him why I wanted to come? I mean—"

"You mean that your feelings were deeply hurt because your father's agent happened also to be your close personal friend?"

"He shouldn't have brought John into it," Jenny said quickly.

"So that's his name, is it? Well, I dare say John will keep for another day."

"But I don't want—" She broke off.

He glanced at her and saw that her lips were pressed together. There was a bright, but not kind light in her eyes.

Jenny slumped down in her seat. Out of the corner of her eye she saw that he had seen that silly gesture of rebellion. She sat up again quickly.

"Did you slip on something?" he asked. He hadn't turned his head, but there was a small and very kindly smile on his lips. Jenny sighed. She couldn't tell him all about it, of course. She couldn't let John down that way. She owed him something—years of family friendship, if nothing else.

Gently, so as not to be noticeable, she lifted herself even higher in her seat. Her back was very straight now. With some effort she brought liveliness back into her manner, too.

"About Nicole," she said brightly, changing the subject, "I think she's wonderful, working to preserve an old ghost town like this one you were talking about. She's a very effective personality, too, isn't she? Very efficient. And reliable. I mean she's not the riding-helter-skelter-over-tree-studded-hills type, is she? Or the kind of girl to walk down old mine shafts—What I mean is that you're lucky to have her on the female side of this safari. She is really *experienced*. Of course I will take your advice, Drew."

He glanced round at her again. He had what Jenny termed a "funny" expression on his face. She was not prepared to like it, not one bit.

So she met his eyes—nonchalantly, in fact. She knew what she would do later, when they got to a sizable town. She'd do some shopping. She'd get herself some sophistication, too!

Her chin was up and her head in the air. In a moment she would start admiring the scenery, even if it was wild, uncannily desolate scenery. She would, in this subtle way, show him that the conversation of before was *closed*.

The silence as they swished, rumbled, and dusted their way over the long, long track became so extended that it was Jenny, without meaning to, who gave in first.

She glanced at him sideways, ever so surreptitiously. He turned his head again and glanced at her, too. Then he looked back again at the track. They were travelling slowly now.

"In my own peculiar fashion I've been telling you this is a cruel country, Jenny—if you're no friend to it. If you love it, you'll learn how to best it. But that will take time. So don't get lost in it. If you stray, lose your direction, or are doubtful, stay under the shade of a straggly mulga. It will befriend you until someone comes. Never leave a shady tree in these parts. Let help come to you. Don't go looking for it."

Jenny was silent a minute.

"Thank you for the lecture," she said at length. "That was what it was, wasn't it? I *am* grateful. I'll remember what you said. But—"

"Yes? But what?"

"I won't get lost."

"Not if you stick around," he said, this time with a grin. "Don't run out on us because you've lost your favorite bush brumby or have pity on a bird with a broken wing. Keep alongside your own kind. That's what the kangaroos were doing, wasn't it? Which one of them first started that big run we saw a mile back? Only God knows. But the rest of them, born and bred in the country, went too, didn't they? And they weren't running out there on the far side where there is only shadeless spinifex, were they? Not on your life. The whole batch of them were sticking to the mulga. Thin shade, but nevertheless *shade*. And they were together."

It was funny, Jenny thought, but Drew's conversation had an effect on her. Quite a deep one, too. It wasn't just the words of wisdom. It was the quiet way he said them. Obey the rules, and the bush—this harsh, dry, claypan scrub—would be your friend. Man, with brain power that could take him to the moon, still had something to learn from the bush in the far reaches of this semi-desert country. And Drew knew it.

There was something else, too. He knew she had run out on a situation at home that she had thought had become intolerable. And he was saying, in effect: *Don't do that again.* This time she had been lucky, but next time Lady Luck might be on the other side of the fence.

9

Pete, when at last they came to his camp, was a joy to behold. Jenny forgot her woes about the Big Boss Fella and his methods of "low cunning."

The earth around was red-red between the tufts of blue grass and the shadows of distant mallee-growth gum trees. All the world seemed empty, uninhabited, except for two things. One was an old, dried-out, burnt-brown man standing beside a windlass. This windlass was attached to a derrick above a hole in the ground. The other object was a Mercedes Benz. It was dusty, but still had the gleam of glamour about it.

It surely couldn't belong to that strange, bow-legged dusty-booted, shabby and bearded old man! Jenny's heart dropped a little. The only person she knew west of the wattle country who owned a Mercedes Benz was Nicole. But Nicole hadn't been on the track out from Coolgardie. She hadn't even been coming this way. Well, not as far as Jenny knew.

How funny-peculiar, she thought, as Drew pulled up some twenty yards from the shaft and its derrick. She guessed what the hole in the ground was. It was collared by a heap of red-white rubble and sand. And it was surmounted by a timber head-frame and windlass. A lone worker's mine! That hole wouldn't take more than one man; it was too small. This strange weathered old man must be Pete the prospector, then. There was no one in the Mercedes Benz. And no one other than the old prospector was in sight. She hadn't remembered Nicole's registration number.

Drew opened his drive door and said, "Come and meet Pete."

"Is he a hermit?" Jenny asked, opening her own door and slipping out.

"No, not quite."

They walked towards the mullock heap. "Saturday and Sunday find him all day in Coolgardie telling yarns of the old days," Drew added. "If he's in the right mood he's the best yarn-spinner this side of the Nullabor."

"The car. That car over there. It's like—"

"It *is* Nicole's car. She's made time enough to come across country to speak to old Pete."

Jenny was puzzled.

"But the track was single-width! She didn't pass us."

She caught an odd expression on Drew's face. It was not a smile; yet the lines between his eyes could not be called a frown. It was something of both: quietly smiling and quietly frowning. In his own mysterious way was he double thinking?

Of course, she did want to be interested in what Pete the Prospector was doing. But she also wanted to know how Nicole had come here, and arrived first, too!

Drew was a mind reader. Jenny decided this, now and for all time.

"Nicole did not come cross bush or through a claypan," Drew said. "Not by the look of her car. She must have done the twenty odd miles into Kalgoorlie to do some shopping and then taken a side-track off the main road to Pete's residence. She'll be there right now, tidying up for him."

"Residence?" Jenny asked, puzzled.

"Not a Governor's residence, by any means," Drew said dryly. "Not even a homestead, by your standards. Be polite to Pete, and he'll take us over. Then you'll see it for yourself."

They had arrived at the shaft. Drew was still speaking, but Pete took not one atom of notice. Bent almost double, he went on shaking a pan. Every now and again he stopped to squeeze a small shabby pair of bellows over the pan's contents. The red dust wafted up in a train of cloudlets, then scattered away into the bush.

Drew dug his hands in his pockets and watched. No one spoke. Jenny was fascinated—not only by what the old man was doing, or by his quaint, shabby, patched clothes and burnt-brown appearance, but also by the fact that he *had* to know they were standing within two yards of him yet he took not the slightest notice.

It seemed ages before he dispatched the last of the dust, shook the pan, then set it down on the mullock heap. Finally he looked up at Drew.

"Heard you were coming through," he drawled. His eyes were a faded blue, and narrowed.

"Nicole told you?"

"I heard you was coming before I saw her. An' I didn't see you down in the pub in town—so it musta been the crows or the 'roos shooting through tellin' me. You oughta seen them go. You kill any one of 'em on your way up, Drew?"

"Nary a one," Drew said.

"They musta known it was you coming, an' kept clear uv the road," the old man said dryly. "See you've got a girl with you. What's this one? Another tourist?"

"No. She's a rouseabout. And a good one."

Jenny silently thanked Drew for that. Perhaps he was only being loyal to his employees, but it was something pleasant to hear it.

There'd been no formal introductions yet. Jenny supposed Drew was biding his time. So she in her turn bided, too, and smiled when the old man looked hard at her. He wiped his hand round his chin and said, "Gor' blimey. Look at them blue eyes. Where'd you catch her, Drew?"

Drew ignored this. Jenny could not help a smile of pleasure. She was glad about her eyes, but more so because Drew was hearing something nice about her from someone else.

"You have some specimens for me, Pete?" Drew asked, his hands still in his pockets and his long legs rocking slightly back on their heels. "Over at the residence?"

"Yeah."

"Nicole over there?"

"Yeah. Making a cup of tea by this time." The old man gave a hint of a grin, then added: "Turning over them specimens for a look-see, I guess."

Jenny, fascinated by this laconic, shorthand conversation between the two men, remained silent. It seemed—out here on the patch—that words were more precious than precious gems.

"Never seen you dry-blowing an old mullock heap before, Pete," Drew said.

"You never seen me all the time," Pete said. "Gotta get out an' find something to do when a female comes in my residence an' starts takin' over."

"Have you found anything?"

"Nary a speck. Didn't expect to. Jes' waiting around."

"For me?"

The old man wiped his hand round his chin again.

"Well, apart from what the crows an' the 'roos were telling me—when that dandy-looking female of yours turned a corner, I sez, 'Hallo, Hallo! Next'll come Drew. I'll jes' hang around an' wait.' "

This was Pete the Prospector's longest speech so far. But the wonder of its length didn't so much affect Jenny as its content. It was full to the brim with information. In *her* shorthand it said that, wheresoever Nicole went, Drew went, too. And vice versa. She didn't wonder why it made her feel smaller than small. She just wondered why her heart dropped. She had decided, a few miles back along the track, not to like Drew very much. So why worry now?

Well, Nicole would not only outshine her—an uncomfortable state for any girl to find herself in—but Nicole would be in charge. Nicole would give the instructions. Nicole would feel at home with Drew in the old prospector's residence. Nicole might somehow subtly cause Jenny to feel the intruder. Or was she, Jenny, afraid of this, and so day-dreaming it into a reality?

And why did she care, anyway? Was she even being fair?

Mystery, mystery!

A shadow passed through the distant grove of trees. The blue grass ruffled before a waft of breeze. The treetops parted and beyond them, between the moving branches, was a distant, low, blue hill very like the hills of home.

For some illogical reason Jenny thought of Redcoat. And suddenly there was mist in her eyes.

Over the hills and far away! That was where she had wanted to go. But heartache was here, too!

A smallish, brown dog with yellow patches on its sides appeared through the blue grass and raced up to the old prospector. Still attentive to Drew, not looking at the dog, the old man bent and patted the dog's head.

"Two things always faithful to you," Pete said, interrupting Drew in the middle of one of his shorthand sentences. "Yer horse and yer dog. They kinda like you, warts an' all. No matter what kind uv a drongo you be, they stick it out with you."

A horse and a dog! Jenny thought. She looked hard at the ground as if she too might find one golden speck left over from Pete's dry-blowing.

"What about that cup of tea? And those specimens?" Drew asked.

"Yep. Guess we'd better get goin'," Pete said. "Till that girl of yours, Drew, cleans me residence up—*her* way—I got nowhere decent to sleep. But maybe we can stake out that cuppa tea. Let's give it a go, eh?"

10

Pete's "residence" was a wonder to behold.

It was a nest of corrugated-iron, shed-like shacks. Some of the iron sheets were rusted and hung together on bent nails pinned to slim but ancient tree trunks. Here and there hessian patches covered what might be a hole, or maybe a make-do window that had never seen glass. In front of the largest shack, slabs of timber uprights had been dug into the ground. Over these slabs was a roof of chicken wire covered with creepers and some rough thatch. Under this creepered shade area stood several rickety and ancient armchairs, very much in the precarious state of barely remaining upright. Nearby, a giant storage barrel leaned at an appropriate angle. A piece of rusted corrugated iron made do as a lid. A sentinel-like, handmade piece of piping thrusting upwards served as a chimney, this contraption being necessary for the burning of waste.

Several shortened tree limbs leaned against one of the shack's walls for the obvious purpose of preventing the wall from collapsing altogether. Against another wall, the one by the thatch-shade, rested a conglomeration of utensils. There were tools, iron pots, billy cans, old boxes, a wreck of a tin trunk, and other unidentifiable objects to which Jenny could put no name.

As soon as Pete put his feet inside his shack he uttered a minor blasphemy.

"Now where the hell 'm I goin' to find a damn thing? Tidy me up, hey? Put everything away when I can't find 'em, hey?"

Nobody would know, looking at Nicole, that she had

done even an hour's clean-up work. She was spotless in a pale blue, tailored, crimplene dress, her hair dressed as if less than two minutes ago she had brushed it and hand-pressed it into order. Her face was made up and pink-powdered, her eyes mascaraed, her lips delicately rouged.

Perhaps all done at the first distant sound of Drew's coming?

So why not?

Jenny wished she could look like that, and felt guilty because Nicole was so immaculate. Jenny felt somewhat dishevelled and was sure she looked it.

Drew's smile was only just there, but there was something faintly intimate in it as he looked at Nicole. Was it because he expected her to look like this and to have done a stout job of clearing up old Pete's place for him? Or was it just his way of showing he was pleased to see her, though they'd been parted for only a few hours?

Nicole did not quite ignore Pete's grumpy ingratitude. Clearly she knew the old man and how to handle him. Nor was she disturbed by the string of expletives that followed as he started searching for something he did not name. Clearly he was making a point that he could not find it because Nicole had tidied it away somewhere.

"Now, no nonsense, Pete," Nicole said very firmly. "At least this place will be clean enough to pass muster for the health authorities from the Shire Offices. It's not the first time I've saved you from being shooed off the area. You know perfectly well squatters aren't allowed near the big towns unless they can prove they're professionally engaged in prospecting, and are not a health hazard to themselves or to other people in the district."

"Well, I'll be—" Pete began.

Drew interrupted him: "—hanged! And well you might be. That is, if you start shooting anything more than game. Maybe a galah to cook along with a stone in the pot? Just appear to be grateful, even if you are not."

"I heard you coming. The billy's on the fire," Nicole said with a smile in Drew's direction. She turned to Jenny. "Do you know what to do with a billy, Jenny? Gum leaves on the top to keep the tea from smoking. I'll hand it over to you. After all, you *are* the cook and rouseabout."

Her eyebrows had gone up in an interesting way. Her smile was quite charming, but Jenny feared this was Nicole's clever way of putting the cook-rouseabout in her proper place.

Ah well! That's what she was. That was the job she had taken.

"Yes, of course," she said, looking around. "But where is the fire and the billy-on-the-boil?"

"Out at the back. Where else?" Nicole was still smiling as if dealing with a child. She spoke extra-kindly as she added: "once out of the southwest forest country, you are very inexperienced, aren't you, Jenny?"

"Yes. But not about *how* to boil a billy. Or about the gum leaves on top. We have bush picnics down south, too. I guess it's an old Australian custom." A new thought struck her. "Where is Geoff?" she asked anxiously. "Didn't he get back from Kalgoorlie?"

Nicole smiled in the way that an older person smiles when about to bestow surprises of a cheerful nature on the young.

"Yes, he did. He has a surprise for you. I do hope it will be a pleasant one. Though how you will manage with two of them in tow, I'll never guess."

"*Two?* Them?" Jenny was puzzled. She glanced round. Where was Drew?

He was in a lead-off room from the main shack, looking at the gemstones Pete had picked up on his prospecting trips.

There was no hope there, Jenny could see that. She was on her own as far as Drew was concerned. She would have to make her own way in this duet of wits with Nicole.

Or was it a battle? She wondered. If so, she thought

she could see why. Nicole had *almost* everything: beauty, glamour, riches, a Mercedes Benz. The only thing she didn't have was something Jenny did. And that was real youth. So Jenny would have to pay. To Nicole, ten years older, Jenny, was the butterfly emerging from the chrysalis and so had to be watched. She might turn into a rival!

"*Two* of them?" she said. "Two of what? I mean, is Geoff bringing someone or something?"

"That would be spoiling it, if I told." Nicole was wearing that odd smile again, and arched eyebrows again, too.

Drew came back into the main room.

"How goes the billy?" he asked. He was examining something in his hand as he moved. "You might have struck it, Pete," he said over his shoulder. "I'd need to play the ultra-violet rays on it to be sure. But I think we might have hit a patch."

He half-turned and looked at Nicole. "This specimen is a real beauty," he said, with a real smile this time. "I think your judgment was right, Nicole." He did not appear to notice Jenny. Jenny, not feeling wanted, moved off to the campfire outback and the boiling billy.

Oh well! I *am* the cook, she thought. I'd better get to it and be a good one. At least making tea out of a tin billy, gum leaves and all, won't be expected to be Codon Bleu.

She picked up an iron bar from the ground and used it to remove the billy to a nest of stones, stained dark from long years of such use. "If only Geoff would hurry up and come." Her sense of humour came to her rescue. "Who would ever have thought I'd be longing for Geoff's company? That is for any reason other than one more argument!"

And yet she was. She not only wanted Geoff. She *needed* him.

The very thought brought a shine to her eyes.

Jenny when she laughed too much often had tears in her eyes. She had no idea why nature had played this strange trick on her. Sometimes it was embarrassing.

These were laughter tears now—and were rather lovely.

The billy safely lodged on its base of stones, Jenny wiped the back of her hand across her eyes and searched in her pocket for a handkerchief. She heard the crunch of boots behind her but was too concerned with the ignoble task of wiping the laughter tears from her eyes to be concerned about which of them had come out. It was probably only to see if she performed the simple job of pouring tea from a billy with good management.

"So there you are, Pesty! Earning your daily dollar while Drew and Nicole are working out the millions they might make from Pete's find? Been a good girl?"

"Oh Geoff!" She was so pleased to see him she could not hide it. "Am I glad to see you! That pair—meaning Drew and Nicole—just about get me tied up in knots."

"What, *you*? The hurry-up girl from Nob's Hill? I'd have to see it to believe it. Meantime, guess what?"

Jenny, now dry-eyed, pushed her handkerchief deep in her pocket and looked at Geoff. "You tell me," she said. "I know we're going north—up the ghost-town way—instead of east. That's knowledge, Geoff, not guesswork. I heard them saying so inside—"

She broke off. Geoff was shaking his head.

"Tell me!" she demanded.

"You have a visitor. All the way from Yaraandoo."

"Don't be silly, Geoff. Nobody in Yaraandoo knows where I am. I told the parents I'd send them a telegram from Denong Outpost and we haven't reached Denong Outpost yet."

"No. But I have. There and back in a day."

"*Please*, Geoff. Don't be so maddening!" Jenny nearly stamped her foot. "What are you talking about?"

He paused to hold her tantalized before he broke the news.

"Promise not to take off on wings of song. I'm getting used to having you around, Pesty. What with Drew and Nicole all but in a twenty-four-hour clinch, I'd be lonely without you. Even if it's only as a sparring partner."

Jenny stooped, picked up a gum nut, and threw it at him. She really stamped her foot this time.

"Who?" she demanded.

"Who else but—are you waiting for it? Well, here it comes. John-o. Old Faithful himself. All the way from Yaraandoo to check—" He broke off, then asked a shade more quickly: "Say, Jenny, what's up?"

Jenny's hand dropped by her side. She caught her bottom lip between her teeth.

Geoff stopped teasing. He took one stride towards her and put his arm round her shoulder. "You all right?" he asked, puzzled.

Jenny was stricken.

Her blue-blue eyes had never seemed to Geoff to be more beautiful. From early youth he'd taken them for granted. They stared at him now, right into his own eyes. They had a kind of pain in them. Then there was a kind of pain in *his* eyes, too.

Both his arms went round her.

"Jenny? What goes? You look as if something's hit you."

Her face had something wooden in it as she stared back at him.

Heavy footsteps could be heard coming from the shack. They now came to a halt. Jenny neither heard nor cared. She was trying desperately hard not to put her head on Geoff's shoulder and cry.

Not John, she was saying inside herself. Not John. I ran away. And—

Drew quietly turned on his heel and went back to the shack.

"I think our tea seems to be taking quite a while to reach the mug stage," he said to Nicole, raising his eyebrows.

Pete peered into the backyard through the gap between the sheet of galvanized iron.

"That's them young things for you," he said. "A plurry love scene going on and us waiting fer our tea.

Thought you said you'd hired yerself a rouseabout, Drew."

Nicole walked past Drew to Pete's side. She, too, peered outside. Her smile when she turned round was almost knowing.

"I did warn you not to take on someone so *young*, Drew," she said. "What with one young man here and another waiting for her at Kalgoorlie you're likely to have trouble on your hands. I did have an informed hunch about that girl when you pulled in at the roadhouse. Just something about her. Now what are you going to do? We can't possibly keep her, of course. We'd be asking for trouble."

Drew's eyes met hers in a thoughtful way.

"I think we'll wait and see," he said very quietly.

Nicole shurgged. "So be it," she said. "But if there's any nonsense, you'd better let me handle it. After all, I am a woman, and managing these things *can* be a problem."

"Thank you, Nicole."

"Well, dernation take them!" Pete said, loud and determined. "I want my tea and I'm going right out an' get that billy. Those cooing drongos can go get their own down at the creek—if they like it cold and muddy thataways."

Nicole put the last of Pete's few possessions away on tidied shelves.

"Really, Drew!" she said, determined patience in her voice. "You are paying that girl to do her job."

"I haven't paid her yet."

"For goodness sake!" Nicole turned and looked at Drew with raised eyebrows. "She hasn't done anything yet. So far, it's been a safari trip with top-grade accommodation laid on free."

"From Kalgoorlie on she'll be different, won't she?"

Nicole was indignant. "You sound as if you're defending her. Are you?"

"From what? From whom?" Drew asked. This time it was *his* eyebrows that were raised enquiringly.

Nicole, still impatient, avoided meeting his eyes.

"Here comes Pete with the billy," she said. "I'll put out the mugs."

"Thank you, Nicole. You're probably the most dependable person on earth," Drew said quietly.

Nicole smiled, and her face softened. To Nicole there was something meditative in the amused expression in Drew's eyes as he looked at her. It pleased her. She walked across the earth floor and clasped her hands around the the back of his neck.

"For a very exacting man with a deceptively quiet manner who is sometimes a bully in a subtle way," she said, deliberately smiling into his eyes, "you can be rather a pet if you try." She kissed him first on one cheek, then on the other. "You're being chivalrous about that girl, which is very sweet of you. But—"

"Yes? But?"

Geoff Hallam stood aside to let Jenny through the shack's opening. She saw Drew and Nicole together. And she saw the two kisses. It bothered her, even more than the fact that John Downing—Old Faithful, as Geoff had called him—had tracked her down.

Kissing in public? she wondered.

Ah well! she consoled herself. It's bad manners, anyway.

11

Next morning it was goodbye to Pete's mullock heap and rickety windlass. Goodbye to old Coolgardie, too.

"What a lovely town it must have been, once, long ago!" Jenny was back as passenger with Geoff again.

"The golden years!" Geoff said. "Here's where they first struck gold. So it was boom town all right, till Paddy Hannan turned up a gold-riddled boulder twenty miles further east. That was the real beginning of the Golden Mile."

"Yes, I read about it in school books."

"Well, it's booming again now. Quite a town!"

"The gemstone boom, and now gold again," Jenny added. "And opal?"

Geoff glanced at her. "We having a competition, or just a quiz show?" he asked.

"A bit of both." Jenny laughed up at him. He grinned back at her.

The old-world beauty of ghost-town Coolgardie had temporarily taken her mind from John and the fact that somewhere round the main street along the Golden Mile he might be on the lookout for her.

"I think Coolgardie's Old Court House is more beautiful than any building down south. Its almost majestic, isn't it? And way out here in the wild country! Like a sort of miracle. Thoses arches! I wonder what sort of architecture the experts call it."

"Early Colonial will do for you and me," Geoff said. "The place I like best is the old Denver City Hotel. I like the shade of those super verandas for having a real-tuck-in with the once-famous Hannan's beer."

"The wide, wide street," Jenny said in wonder. "The widest ever."

"When they built this place—and Kalgoorlie, too—they built the streets wide enough to turn around the camel trains."

"I know. I've read about that. Wouldn't it have been wonderful to be alive in those days? The Afghan traders, the miners pushing their barrows. Everyone struggling and pushing to get first to the next water hole. And the rushes! Everyone lining up and starting the race at the shot of the starter's gun."

"You'd be dead and buried by now, Jenny. That is, if you'd lived in those days. Now you're hale and hearty, with John-o waiting up the road for you." He looked at his speedometer. "Sixteen miles to go."

"Will you please stop calling him John-o? You only do it to annoy me."

Geoff's grin was at its maximum.

"Put your ruffles down, bratto," he said. "I'm not hurting your best beloved boy friend. I'm only being affectionate."

Jenny was on the point of saying something tart. She was restrained by the fact that Geoff had to make a fast swerve as a long, low, blue car shot past on the overtake at an ungodly speed.

"Guess Nicole'll turn herself over in that Mercedes Benz one day," he said dryly. "Funny how when people've got posh cars they make 'em sing so everyone will take notice."

It was Jenny's glance to turn sideways.

"You don't like her then?" she asked tentatively.

"Oh—she's okay. A bit possessive where the boss is concerned."

"But, if he likes it?"

"He'd have to, wouldn't he? Otherwise he wouldn't go for it, would he?"

Jenny was thoughtful. "I suppose you're right," she said at last.

She stared thoughtfully out of the window. "Those old mines," she went on sadly, looking at the derricks in the distance. "All that old machinery. And those huge mullock heaps. Such a waste!"

"Useful tourist attractions," Geoff said bluntly.

They were back in the wild country now. Over the claypans and far away! Jenny thought. Nowadays, people might stop at Coolgardie to refuel their cars, snatch a meal, and take a quick, wondering look around as they shot through. Then it was usually out and away to wherever it was they were going: Kalgoorlie and the Golden Mile, north to Leonora, or perhaps northeast to the Gibson Desert, where they actually grew millions and millions of melons, thanks to the underground water.

Strange, strange, wonderful land! It was really getting to her. The long, straight road stretched ahead. On either side, as far as she could see, was this near-desert, blue-grass country that looked as if it went on for ever, reaching for a horizon it too would never meet.

"It's so mysterious, isn't it?" she said. "Why should such an empty, flat, desolate land be mysterious?"

"You waxing poetical, or something?" Geoff asked dryly.

"No. But maybe I'm feeling like it."

"Well, let's talk about something else, because this is nothing to what you'll strike once we head north."

"All right. Change of subject," Jenny said. "Where is Drew? And why didn't he come with us?"

"Because he went out with old Pete the Prospector to look at that patch Pete was talking about. You wouldn't catch Drew missing out on a find. Not if an old, experienced prospector like Pete and he had something up his sleeve."

"Thank you. Curiosity on that point satisfied. Now for the next question. Why did you really go to Kalgoorlie yesterday? Is there something special going on? Sort of confidential?"

"If there is, then that's the way it has to stay. Right?"

"Oh Geoff, you really are aggravating. I suppose

you're right. Except that—why do I have to be kept out?"

"If you don't know the X factor involved in this safari, you can't tell anyone else about it, can you?"

"What about yourself?" Jenny demanded indignantly.

"I've worked with Drew on one of his safaris before, remember? That's how I came to know Nicole. He knows he can trust me."

"And doesn't think he can trust *me*?" Jenny was twice as indignant as she had been a moment before.

"Why should he? And then again, why should he not? Answer: because he doesn't know you. He sees you as the kid sister of the organization—someone who has to be wrapped in cotton wool, taken care of, watched over. Guess he's not keen on that John-o of yours turning up. Not that he knows anything about said John-o, except for what Nicole may have said."

Jenny remained silent. She could see the point, but this didn't stop her feeling hurt somewhere deep inside her. Why should it matter whether or not Drew took precautions about her? She didn't know. She wished she did. She wished she knew what the X factor Geoff had mentioned really was. She felt a mystery in her bones. It reminded her of the feeling she had had on seeing that strange man with the white hat waiting in the shadows of the bush by the roadhouse. Why had he been standing there at that odd hour of the morning? But mainly she wished she had made such a good impression on Drew that he could have trusted her at first glance. Oh, how she wanted to know all that the others seemed to know!

"Talking about mollycoddling"—Geoff interrupted her thoughts. "Yesterday's problem for Drew was to locate some suitable accommodation for you. I found it: a dandy motel on the south-side boundary of the Golden Mile. Quite a place."

"For me?" Jenny was not impressed. She was on safari, wasn't she? She wanted to be with the others.

"Where are the rest of you staying?" she asked.

"Nicole the Pathfinder has gone ahead to follow through on reports of some vague byway track that will get us a short cut through via Barrett's station boundary. That'll be a port of call some time, I guess. Me, I'm dumped in a sleeping bag in the back of Drew's Land Cruiser. This here four-wheel drive will take a rest and I'm sort of it's caretaker. As for Drew—well, honey, Drew's for the Palace Hotel which is quite a place. Famous. That's where the geologists, prospectors, boys from the Mining Press, and of course the mining spies—all dressed up like the gentlemen they aren't—nest out, mostly in the plush downstairs bar, known as the hot spot in the gold fields for picking up the gossip. Who's found what, and where. You know something?"

"No, you tell me." Jenny was still feeling left out from some kind of notable adventure.

"Last time I was on a safari trip with Drew, in that same Palace Hotel bar," Geoff went on, "we were all packed in like sardines and having a peaceable drink when indoors come the dustiest old prospector you ever saw. Wide-awake brown hat still on, and caked with bush grime and mud dust. Whiskers half a foot long. He said nary a word but slapped down on the counter the biggest nugget of pure gold you ever saw. Girl, was there a scramble! The mob drowned him with free drinks—anything to get information out of him!"

"And did they?"

"Not a word. He'd clean forgotten the English language." Geoff laughed. "He was an old hand at not being caught that way. Leastwise, so Drew said."

"And Drew was part of all this?"

"Drew? He sat in one of those plush velvet corner seats and watched. Just watched. Drew's a downy bird, Jenny, and he'd learn more that way than all the rest of them put together."

"But what did he want to learn? I mean, he's just looking for opal and gemstones, isn't he? Or isn't he?"

"You ask him that one yourself some day, Jenny. But choose your time. And mighty carefully, too. Like

I said, Drew seems a nice, quiet, kind guy on the surface. But underneath? Oh, boy! There's deep fires! That is, when there isn't a deep freeze."

Yes, Jenny thought, sinking a little lower in her seat. That's what I thought myself, almost from the first day.

But she said nothing.

They were entering Kalgoorlie now and the best thing she could do was to watch out for a car with a YO country number on the back. Then she'd know just whereabouts it was that John was on the lookout for her.

How she remembered that car number! And how the thought of it now sent her spirits down into the darker glades of something without any name she could put to it.

Then she saw it.

A dark grey Holden, the black registration number dusted over on the white reflection plates, but nevertheless unmistakable—it was parked outside one of the lesser hotels. It had come the long distance, probably nonstop, because John was the sort of person who always kept his car immaculate if he had any time at all to do so. Even after the shortest drive out to a farm on business he had the hose, then the duster, over the car, shining it up. But right now it looked as if he had not had the chance to do any cleaning.

There was no one in the car.

Jenny glanced quickly at Geoff, but Geoff had his eyes straight ahead watching for the turn-off that would take him to the motel.

She said nothing. There was nothing she *could* say, because she couldn't even think straight. Inside her something was crying, Oh, no! *No!* That was all. She could put no words to her feelings. They didn't make sense, even to her. They were just feelings, nothing more. She simply *felt* quite dreadful—like a fugitive, someone who wanted to run for it and couldn't because wherever she ran to, *it* would be there!

Geoff was right about the motel. It was so spanking-new that Jenny blinked at it. Inside, it was like most motels, except that everything was not only new but *smelt* new. It was fresh-paint smell. Her room had a double bed and a single bed, like most of them had, and its own bathroom. There was a small fridge, and a hot-water jug on the top of a waist-high cupboard. Inside the cupboard, she knew there'd be two cups and saucers, two tumblers, a jar with packets of tea and coffee and sugar. The tiny fridge would hold a jug of fresh milk.

On the wall opposite the window there was an air-conditioner. Geoff switched it on to a pleasant 20°C. He put her case on the low rack meant for such purposes.

"All set, serene, cool, and comfortable!" he said with a grin. "I'll have to leave you now, Jenny. Have to park the flaming Land Rover some place safe, then make for the good old Palace Hotel and wait for Drew. If you want anything, just lift the telephone and the entire eastern gold fields will be yours for the calling. Okay?"

For once Jenny, who had so often longed to be alone, thought that being alone was worse than being ill. She felt deserted. She hadn't known she could ever want company so much.

That was the first time she thought of them—Drew, Nicole, and Geoff—as the "Council of Three." She herself, of course, was the lone outsider.

"Geoff—?"

He had reached the door.

"Want something?" he asked.

He was willing and able, she knew. But he couldn't give her what she wanted. Which was—at the moment—*not* to be dumped. Just to be one of them.

I asked for it, she thought. I wanted to run away to be myself. Now I've done it; and this is what it's like. Lonely.

"Geoff, *please*! Don't make wisecracks or be funny-funny. Because I mean it."

He looked at her in surprise. She guessed what he

was thinking. Where was our Jenny-run-quickly who could go any place, any time—and with all the confidence in the world?

Before him was a rather travel-tired, dusty girl, her hair just that much dust-blown that it wouldn't obey when she tried to throw it over her shoulder. The blue eyes were not so blue, either. They were troubled and hiding anxious thoughts.

"Okay, Pesty," he said quietly, and sat down on the double bed beside her. "I won't crack funnies; so let's have it. What goes?"

She looked away for just a fraction of a minute, because she didn't really *want* to ask him what she was about to ask him. Yet she must, old friend and foe that he had been over the years.

"Geoff—" Her eyes actually pleaded. "If you see John, please don't tell him where I am.

Geoff's eyebrows went up. He was surprised and wasn't hiding it.

"Not tell him? You mean that, Jenny? Hellfire and mad kangaroos! He's come darn near a thousand miles to catch up with you. His girl friend—"

"Geoff, I can't say *why*. It's personal. It's all over with John, and it can't start again. Not now. Please, Geoff, I can't talk about it, and you know I can't. I mean—it's not done, is it? I mean—*noblesse oblige,* and all that?"

Geoff uncrossed, then crossed his long legs. Jenny sat very still beside him. He put his arm around her gently. To her it was heaven.

"What goes?" he said. "You really can't tell your old Uncle Charlie?"

"I wish you were my Uncle Charlie. Then I just might. But I can't talk about it." He saw the trouble in her eyes. "You know that, Geoff. If it was you and some girl friend, you wouldn't talk about it, would you?"

"No, I guess not. My next thought is that probably you don't love him. So you're caught in an honour-comes-first play. Don't answer, Jenny; then I won't know, will I? Okay. If I see John and he asks questions, I just don't know the hell about anything or anybody. I'll tell him to go look somewhere on the Gibson Desert, or maybe the Nullabor Plain. They're far away from here."

Jenny shook her head. "Just don't say where I am. That's all. Maybe at the back of your mind you're thinking I'm a little beast. But, Geoff, I can't help it if you do. Maybe that's what I am. But I can't help that either."

Geoff's free hand pressed her head gently against his shoulder. They sat on the bed side by side.

"That's life for you!" he said. "You're not the first who's fallen out of love, and you'll not be the last. Maybe you didn't love him at all? Will it cheer you if I tell you I'm not surprised? Everyone back home thought you were tied in; so I, along with the others, just took it for granted without really thinking about it. But he's not your type, really. Too serious. Never any fun. Too wrapped up in climbing the ladder."

"Please, Geoff, don't say any more. He's a good man. Hard-working, dedicated. Very reliable. It's just that—just that he *never smiles.*"

"What you mean is, he's always *right.* And serious about it. Some people are born that way. You can't have an argument with a fella like that. Not even a frivolous discussion."

"I don't want to hear anything against him, Geoff. I don't want ever to think anything against him. And worst, hardest of all, I don't want to make a fool of him."

"Pesty, you can't. Not with a fella who's always *right.* He's *never* a fool. He's a good know-all man who ought to marry a good know-all girl, and live happily ever after. But a young filly like you? I've been one of a dozen of our pals back at Yaraandoo who thought that way. But we couldn't say it, could we? Meaning no harm to John, it's just the kind of girl you are, Jenny. You've got a dash of spirit. You're a girl for laughs. The best horsewoman in the district. A real champ.

You know what? I'm glad as hell this has come out in the open." He ruffled his hand through her hair. "Not to worry, kiddo; I won't say anything. Fact is, I make a general practice of dodging him. Nothing against old John in that! Just that I always feel I don't measure up; so why try? He's an inch taller than I am, anyway."

"Geoff, you are a dear. Thank you."

Vaguely they had both heard a car pull in fast round the courtyard and come to a sudden smacking halt outside the next-door unit. Neither realized the key was in this door, and that the door had been left unlatched. Each was concerned, at the moment, with the other.

"Thank you," Jenny said again. There were nearly tears in her eyes as she put her arms round Geoff and kissed him. Somehow that was solace, a sort of heavenly solace. Dear Geoff.

The sound of a knock, then of the door being flung open, startled them.

Nicole was standing there.

"Oh dear!" she said in a resigned way. "This is what it's all about, is it? Both from the same town. I didn't think it was wise in the first place. There was, unfortunately, a staff shortage."

With one hand Geoff deliberately kept Jenny's arm locked round his neck, yet free enough so that he could turn his head.

"I thought you were supposed to be off on some way-out track looking for a short cut," he said mildly. For Jenny's sake, he didn't say, "Take off!" It was the first time in his life he had so disciplined himself.

"So I was, but I'm back. Probably just as well." Nicole clearly had nasty ideas about Jenny and Geoff billing and cooing on a double bed in a motel room. "I don't know what Drew will say about Jenny entertaining you in her room. There are certain safari rules—" She broke off.

"If you have one sacked, you have two sacked, Nicole," Geoff said dryly, deliberately keeping Jenny's arms pinned around him. "Shortage of staff? Poor

Drew. You almost make me sorry for him. And another thing—"

Nicole's eyebrows were almost at her hairline. "Yes?" she asked coldly.

"A rule for one is a rule for all. You're covered, too."

Nicole couldn't find words. She was white with anger. She turned on her heel, went out, and did not close the door softly.

"Geoff, you are not very chivalrous!" Jenny said with a hiccup. Then suddenly they were both laughing. They flung themselves backwards, their heads resting side by side on the far edge of the bed, and laughed and laughed.

"Golly gosh!" Geoff said at last. "I guess the sun's come out again, hey?"

"And shining bright and clear!" Jenny agreed.

"Then up. Get yourself a shower, change your dress, and make a cup of tea. All's well in a reasonably good world; so let's get on with the safari!"

"Right!" Jenny trilled the "r" with glee. She felt like a different person.

"Meantime I'm up and off to the Palace in search of Big Boss Fella," Geoff said. "If I see old John-o cropping grass round the home paddock I'll duck down the nearest alley and get lost."

"Thank you again, Geoff. And please don't call him John-o. His name is John, ending with an 'n.' "

"Still loyal? Ah well, good for you, Jenny. You always were a nice brat, even if I did pull faces at you in the long ago."

"You were nice too, Geoff, even if I did turn my back. Actually—well, its funny, but I was always sorry afterwards. I wonder why?"

Geoff was up and at the door. He waved one hand, ignoring her last remark.

"So long, kiddo," he said. "See you in the morning."

"In the morning," she said, and blew him a kiss. Geoff caught it in air, and with the palm of his hand pressed it hard on his forehead.

"That's for keeps," he said, and was gone.

12

Jenny did not go to the motel dining room for dinner that night. She wasn't hungry, though she knew she should eat something. Today was the last of civilization and its amenities. Tomorrow would start the doing-it-the-hard-way part of the trip. She rang for room service and asked for some cold beef and salad. That was as much as she could manage.

She made herself coffee with the help of the hot-water jug and a packet of coffee from the cupboard below the work bench.

If Geoff, Nicole, and Drew were dining together, she knew now that Geoff would carry a flag for her. He wouldn't let her down even if Nicole took this opportunity to tell Drew of the "goings-on" in Jenny's motel unit. Two alone on a double bed!

Jenny began to laugh at the very thought of it. It was a memory she was sure she would treasure all her life.

The next morning came the early start. Jenny was up at dawn. That meant four-thirty. By five she had had her shower and a quick snack breakfast—again with the help of the hot-water jug, plus a bread roll and a tea bag.

She had packed her carry-all and had barely pulled on her desert boots when a sharp knock came at the door. She hoped it was Geoff and not Nicole.

It was neither. There, standing in the doorway, his stetson clapped down over his brow, his long, slim-trousered legs slightly apart, stood Drew. As it wasn't really light enough yet, Jenny couldn't see whether he

93

was smiling or not. She thought not, but she caught a pale reflection in his eyes. This gave them a steely, stern look.

"Oh, good morning—" Jenny faltered. "Will you come in?"

"No, thank you. We haven't time. Are you ready?"

"Down to the last bobby pin."

"Good." He ignored her attempt at humour. "Better put your hat on now, Jenny. That way you won't forget it. You'll need that hat by midday. Which reminds me—"

He rocked back on his heels ever so slightly. "If we part company in the bush even for a hundred yards, you don't move without your hat on your head and your water bag over your shoulder. Have I told you that before?"

"No. But I knew that rule."

Drew was in a thoughtful silence. Jenny felt uncomfortable. What was on his mind now? They were still standing in the doorway, facing one another. She waited while he marshalled together whatever it was he was about to say. But he didn't say it. Instead, he half-turned away, then remarked over his shoulder, "I can't bring the Land Cruiser in through the motel entrance. It's outside. I'll give you five minutes. Right?"

Jenny's heart did a skip and a jump. So she was going with *him*?

"Four and a half minutes," she said, and turned back into the room. She took one last peek in the looking-glass as she pulled on the cotton hat. She inspected her safari rig-out, including her desert boots. All was well. Then she picked up her carry-all.

She switched off the light and closed the door behind her, leaving the key in the lock as she had been instructed to do by the office girl yesterday.

Drew was striding across the wide gravel square and out under the entrance arch. Jenny half ran and half walked. She had all but caught up with him as he reached the Cruiser.

"Punctual, aren't I?" she said brightly, hoping to break down the solemnity of his manner.

He opened the passenger door for her.

"That's how it has to be from now on," he said briefly as he took her carry-all and pushed it into the back of the Cruiser. He walked round the vehicle, opened the door, and eased himself into the driver's seat.

The dawn was fast changing. First in its strange, other-world way it had become temporarily darker; then, quite suddenly, the sky and all the world became grey. Next everything turned pale grey. Then there was light, just like that.

Drew ran the Cruiser out of town along a gravel track which passed old mine workings and the last of the heaps of rusted iron sheets that meant people once camped here in a semi-permanent way in tin shanties. Some had been miners, some followers, hangers-on, those who could trade in news of finds. Some were even the Afghans who brought in the camel trains and the stores from across the three hundred miles of semi-desert and desert proper.

A dried-out, desolate sadness hung over everything. This was the seared and scattered debris of a time past, the Gold Boom of long ago. Would there be another one? Some people thought so.

Jenny didn't mind the silence as they moved along, twisting here, turning there, to avoid miniature clay-pans, fallen boulders, old mullock heaps. The sky paled. The sparse trees—so few of them—stood there, wiry, enduring. They were like black etchings against the backdrop of the morning sky.

Then to the east—that was Drew's side—the horizon splashed gold. Overhead the sky became a blue haze. The tree trunks and everything in all the land stood still, hushed and still. The low bush, the lonely trees, a kangaroo against the skyline, the lizards, the snakes, the leaves on the boughs—all things that walked or crawled or ran were still. All things that flew or fell—as gums do—were still. Even Drew had cut the

Cruiser's engine, as if he, too, were part of this early-dawn awakening. Its silence was holy.

The hush, Jenny thought, must have been the same on the day when planet Earth was born.

Then, second by second, the golden arc, the edge of a great burnished coin, eased up over the eastern sky-line.

It was day.

Jenny breathed out.

Drew started up the engine again and moved the gear stick. The wheels rolled, and a breeze touched the leaf-tops of the trees. The kangaroo went with its peculiar hopping movement into the underbush. A stick fell from a tree. Gravel spattered sideways from under the car's wheels. A goanna raced through the dried grass.

The work of the world had begun.

Jenny took a deep breath of pure admiration. It was like a long-held sigh.

"So that is dawn in the Outback," she said at last.

Drew did not answer at once.

"Yes," he said, at length. "It is always like that. And at sundown, too. At sundown, everything stops and waits."

"You, too?"

"Yes."

"Why?" Jenny asked gently. She felt as if she were whispering in some church service.

"I don't know," Drew said. "Ask any Outbacker. Maybe it's just the miracle of it. Even Man, for all his wicked ways, doesn't dare to spit in the face of wonder. So he just watches. And waits."

Jenny's heart did strange things. Drew didn't often use such colorful expressions. He was not like Geoff. Geoff's expressions were a kind of vocabulary of his own. But Drew's were something different. Jenny understood them.

She longed to steal a glance at him, but did not dare. He would know it if she did.

"Thank you for booking me in at the motel," she

said, just to bring the conversation back to the mundane. "It was very comfortable."

"Good. Geoff reported favourably."

"All details included? Even down to sitting on the double bed?"

"No. It was Nicole who mentioned the double bed." He was staring straight ahead. His eyes could look into the sun and were actually doing that right now. The track had turned eastwards.

Jenny felt she must keep her head, and the best way to do that was to talk of other things.

"Nicole looked so fresh and—*groomed* when she called in. It's hard to believe she'd come from a long run through the real bush. Why did she go out path-finding yesterday, Drew? Am I allowed to ask? I mean, aren't we taking a well-used track to—wherever it is we're going?"

"No, we're taking an old, seldom-used track. It's little known except to a few prospectors. We'll turn off on to it in about half an hour. It's old station country, mostly eaten out now. No ground scrub. Nicole knew it well when she was a girl. She comes from station people out this way."

"Is that why you use her as navigator?"

"Yes." He was very brief.

Jenny longed to ask him exactly where they were going, meaning where on the map. But she did not dare. Drew was in his withdrawn mood again. An extra sense warned her it would be a far better thing to leave him alone in it than try to beguile him out of it. After all, to Drew, she was only the cook-rouseabout—an unsophisticated bit-piece under twenty years of age at that.

Drew himself broke the silence some long time later.

"We turn west about two hundred yards on," he said. "I think you'd better hold the door handle to keep you steady. It's an old track that has seldom been used. It's mostly overgrown." He was silent again for the space of ten seconds, then added: "That is, according to Nicole's report."

"She has courage to go out there alone."

"Not in a well-equipped car—which is also a well-cared-for car." He was communicative now. She has a two-way radio, and she knows what to do in the Outback if she loses a wheel, loses her way, or finds a brown snake slithering over the back seat."

"You're trying to scare me," Jenny said with a laugh.

He glanced at her. "What would *you* do if any of what I have just described happened to you?" he asked. He appeared to be genuinely curious now, and not merely down-putting.

"Even if I come from the deep south and not the dry Outback?" she said. "In the case of Numbers One and Two, that is a car breakdown, or getting lost, I'd sit and wait in the car. That's another priority rule, isn't it? Never leave your car? It's like a yachtsman in trouble off-shore; he should never try to swim for it. If he stays with the boat, someone will see it—from an airplane, if not from some passing vessel. Number Three about the brown snake? Well, I guess I'd just leave it curled up on the passenger seat, then say my prayers. What else could I do?"

For the first time since he had knocked at her door that morning he really smiled.

"Good girl," he said. "One and Two are right, and as for the brown snake, this is what else you could do. Just let it go to sleep and, when it's good and sound asleep, you use this." He took his right hand from the steering wheel, bent down, and lifted from under his seat a nasty-looking spanner with a heavy claw head. "The only thing to remember is to keep yourself cool and not to miss," he said. "Crack it on the head, and that's all. Its tail will thrash around but its head will be finished—its fangs trapped in the roof of its mouth."

"Thank you," Jenny said. "I'll remember; but I still hope I won't meet a brown snake."

He really grinned. There was something heart-warming in it now.

"You're not likely to meet one," Drew added. "We

don't have them up this way. Only lizards and sand snakes."

Jenny would have liked to hit him. He'd been leading her on!

But she couldn't do anything, he being the boss, as well as the driver. She fell back on silent dignity and sat bolt upright, her chin in the air, her eyes looking straight ahead. She would send him to Coventry! In a few minutes she would pretend to be tired, then make the motions of leaning back, head on the side, and falling asleep. He jolly well could have this long, nasty strip of arid semi-desert to himself!

Jenny hadn't really meant to fall asleep, but she very nearly did. She was saved from this last indignity by an almighty bump that sent the Cruiser into a ricochet off the track into the bush.

Drew slammed on the brake and pulled up mere inches from a dead tree.

Jenny shook herself together.

"A shaft hole!" Drew said, obviously angry. "Why don't they fill the damn things in when they've found it's a no-go try?"

"Perhaps dug fifty years ago?" Jenny ventured.

"Not on your life! This is the new generation of fossikers. The area is already pegged; so it's a legal claim. That hole would be a sneak try by marauders. If you look back you'll see they've covered the hole with bush debris to hide their handiwork."

"Will we come across more of them?"

"Here and there. I suggest we take time off for a tea break," he said. "Billy tea, or coffee from the thermos flask?"

"Billy tea, please. And I'll make it. I mean the fire, and all. That's my job, isn't it?"

That smile of his was there again. Jenny had the feeling he wanted to laugh at her, though not in an unkind way. Oh, if only she weren't a mere eighteen! If she'd been twenty now, or twenty-one, he'd have more

respect for her ability. Why hadn't she put up her age?
She just hadn't thought of it, that was all!

She didn't wait for him to come round the Cruiser
and open the door for her. She had strong, capable
hands and even the heavy double-lock of the Land
Cruiser was easy for her. With a quick flick she had the
door open, had dropped to the ground, and was some
yards away, scooping a hollow in the sand between the
bushes with the heel of her desert boot.

"Don't tell me how to do it, *please*," she begged.
"I've made fires in the forest and billy tea since I was
a child. And we have bushfires down south, too. Whop-
pers. One learns from the time one toddles how to
make a fire that won't spread, that will make coals but
not a blaze."

"Go ahead!" he said coolly. "But don't be so angry
while you're about it. Were you born angry, Jenny?"

She looked up straight into his eyes. There was quite
a silence.

"I think I must have been," she said at length.
"There's something inside me. I don't know what it is.
Restlessness? No. Something more."

"Something different?" he asked.

"I don't know—"

"I didn't mean anything in particular," he said quietly. "Get on with making your kind of fire, Jenny. I'll
get the billy and the tea. It will save time if we both
work."

But he didn't move. Yet he wasn't cheating by
watching to see she made a bush fire safely. He was
watching *her*—in a sort of thoughtful way. When she
looked round, hoping to catch him at it, he wasn't
looking at her any more. His eyes, slitted in that curious way Outback men have when looking into the sun
or sizing up some antagonist, were staring northwards
at the bush. Maybe he was expecting something to
come out of it? Something for which he was waiting?

Was Nicole expected to come back to a rendezvous?
Or even Geoff? The plan had been for Nicole to lead
the way and Geoff, with the main load of stores, to fol-

low her dust. They'd be surely somewhere up there northwards by now.

Jenny made the billy tea—gum leaves and all floating on top to take out the smoky flavour.

When she straightened herself, holding the billy by a stick through the handle in true bushman fashion, she saw that Drew still had not moved. He was standing now, his feet slightly apart, his body subtly balanced between them. He was listening—looking and *listening*. Neither Jenny nor the billy tea existed for him.

Suddenly he came out of his stillness and strode forward. He went about thirty yards into the bush at the side of the track, bent over some low scrub, and lifted a small grey bundle from the foliage.

Jenny put down the billy, billy-stick and all, and ran towards him.

"A joey!" she cried. "A poor little joey!"

It was alive but not very much so. It had taken Drew's bushman's eyes and ears to know something had been there in the bush.

"Let me have it," she begged, holding out her hands.

"Not till we see how it goes. Even at this young age, that right hind leg could turn into a useful claw."

"It's only a baby."

"We'll take it back to the car and see if it needs food."

Jenny's heart was on Drew's side again. He was so careful with the tiny baby kangaroo. It might have been a human child the way he carried it.

"What happened to it?" she asked.

"The mother must have thrown it out of her pouch when she sensed she was in danger," he said.

"Yes, they always do that. Would it be 'roo shooters?"

Drew nodded. "We passed a dead doe back there," he said. "She'd been shot."

Jenny took a carton from the tinned stores in the back of the Cruiser and set it down on the floor by the gear box.

"I'll look after Joey," she said hopefully.

Drew still held the tiny animal in his hands. He looked over his bush burden at Jenny and his eyebrows flickered.

"You take it for granted we're going to keep it!" he said quizzically.

"Well, we're not going to throw it back in the bush, are we?" Jenny demanded. "Else why did you go and save it?"

"Point made," Drew said. "You win. Now for about two ounces of watered-down milk. While you prepare that and cover Joey in the box, I'll go chew grass."

"Chew grass?" Jenny was puzzled. He must be a little mad, although in a nice way, of course.

To her amazement, that was exactly what Drew did do. He scrabbled around for young shoots, shook them dry of bush debris and clay, washed them in water from the reserve can, and then proceeded to chew them thoroughly—till they were reduced to pulp.

Jenny was cradling the joey in her arms. It was very weak, so made little effort to protest.

"Okay," Drew said, coming towards her with a fine mushy pad of chewed grass in the palm of one hand. "Hold the joey in your left arm. That's right. Now cup your right hand over the joey's head and hold it tight. Don't have any mercy and don't let it wriggle. We're about to get on with the business of saving its life. But it doesn't understand that yet. Ready?"

Jenny nodded.

"Now ease your left arm slightly so that your left hand is free but your arm is still holding the creature quiet. Got it?"

Jenny nodded.

"Good. Now keep your right hand holding the head firmly and we'll get to work."

Drew spilled a little watered-down milk down the joey's throat with one hand while he held the mouth open with the other. When he had seen the little animal had swallowed, he put a morsel of his own chewed grass in its throat and poked it downwards with his forefinger.

"Now watch," he said. "If it chews we're saved."

The joey regurgitated and brought the grass pad back into its mouth; then its little jaws began to work. It was more of a suck than a chew.

"Hurray!" Drew said. "It's old enough to eat. That means old enough to be saved."

Jenny's head was bent over the tiny animal. Her eyes, had she known it, or even thought about it, were tender and full of care for the tiny animal. The joey might have been her child.

When she looked up, Drew's eyes were watching her. She had no idea what he was thinking. She only knew she would like this moment to go on for ever.

Which, of course, was ridiculous.

They put the joey back in the box on the floor, cleared up the tea-break mess, checked every inch of the fire area, then hefted themselves back in the Cruiser.

Two hours later, they crossed a grid iron through a wire fence, came through a clearing, and saw Geoff's Land Rover at halt. The huge square hold-all that had been riding on the roof rack was now on the ground. It had been opened, and its contents, a safari frame-tent, were in the process of being rigged up.

"Hiya!" Geoff said, not looking round. "If I let go of this pole, the whole darn thing will collapse."

"Then don't let it go,'" Drew advised bluntly. "Where's Nicole?"

"Up front. She's rigging her own quarters. Can't beat Nicole for knowing how to do things herself, her way, and all *for* herself."

He wasn't being sarcastic. He was just talking through a piece of rope which he was holding between his teeth while he used his two hands to adjust first one pole, then the other—in order to hold up the tent. Jenny had let herself out of the passenger seat and was now bending over as she reached for the joey's box. The passenger door had swung back on its hinges and Geoff, glancing round, did not see her.

The poles were right now, and he took the rope from his teeth and held it taut.

"Where's Jenny?" he asked. There was a note of concern in his voice, as if he feared Drew might have thrown her out for being a nuisance. It quite warmed Jenny's heart to hear it.

Funny! she thought. Geoff Hallam and I close friends! Who'd believe it back in Yaraandoo?

She straightened up with the box in her arms and kicked the door shut with one foot.

"Here I am!" she called. "Me, my little one, and all!"

"What?" Geoff almost yelled. Then he saw the small animal.

"You gave me a ruddy fright," he said roughly.

Drew stood with his feet slightly apart, his hands tucked in his belt. His eyes were expressionless, but watchful. Always watching, Jenny thought.

"That's a good job you've made of the tent," Drew remarked casually. "Must have learned your knot technique canoeing down that creek of yours back in the forest."

"No, I learned it from you. Last time. Remember? What in the name of jumping kangaroos has Jenny got there?"

"Just what you said. Only in the singular. One kangaroo. At the infant stage."

The tent was now secure; so Geoff walked towards them. Jenny held the box in front of her proudly. She could almost have been the joey's mother.

Geoff peered down at the little grey bundle.

"For crying out loud!" he said again, but this time in an exasperated voice. "We're not going to have *that* for a passenger, are we?"

"Ask Jenny," Drew said. He walked away, round Geoff's Land Rover and the tent annex. He was clearly heading in search of Nicole and whatever it was Nicole was doing, ably of course, to her expensive Mercedes Benz.

"Can't get to her quick enough, can he?" Geoff said

with a flick of his head, indicating Drew's retreating figure. He added a bit of extra wickedness to his grin.

"Who the heck's going to look after that thing?" he demanded, looking down at the joey again. "It'll need feeding at least once an hour. Day and night."

"I'll put it by my sleeping bag." Jenny sounded very determined. "If you're so anxious about it, Geoff, you can sleep in the next-door bag and take *your* turn."

"Nice work!" He didn't know whether to tease or be exasperated. Love Jenny, love her joey. There was nothing he could do about either.

13

Nicole had evidently heard the sounds of approach and the call of voices. She came through the network of filigree bush beyond Geoff's Rover and met Drew halfway.

"Hi there, Nicole," Geoff called. "Come look at this thing! Jenny says I can share a pad with her tonight to help with the chores."

Nicole stood still and looked at Drew, eyebrows raised.

"Share a pad? Did *you* hear what *I* heard, Drew? I did warn you about that girl. Too young to know what she's saying, let alone what she's doing."

Drew, hands in his belt again, looked away into the distance, then back to Nicole. His smile seemed to express a disconcerting lack of interest.

"She's eighteen and has a vote," was all he said.

"I suppose you're right." Nicole was very cool now. "We'll have to put up with her quirks for the time being, I suppose. But if we're to have harmony, she'll need a guiding hand."

Drew smiled in a comforting way. "You'll be very good at that, Nicole," he said. "The guiding-hand business, I mean. You have guided us very ably through this side track. For that, many thanks."

She reached up and kissed his cheek. It was a mere peck; yet to the others it seemed loaded.

"You always were a peacemaker." Her voice was dulcet now. "How do you do it?"

"By never letting my left hand know what my right hand is doing."

Nicole laughed. "That's what *you* think!" she said, her head up, challenging him.

Jenny could not lip-read; she could only see Nicole looking upwards, her very attractive face breaking into a smile, and Drew looking down. He, too, was smiling now.

Ah well! Jenny told herself, hugging her little grey joey. I do have something to love, even if it's only a stray kangaroo.

"Talking to yourself?" Geoff asked. "Here, give me the bratto and I'll carry it homeward to the tent while you fetch your carry-all from the 'bus, luv. It looks as if Drew has other things on his mind."

The tent house Geoff had rigged was cunningly designed. A centre canvas wall made it into two tiny rooms under the one roof. One room was for a kitchen; the other became sleeping quarters for the cook-rouseabout—Jenny. Nicole had her own canvas affair rigged onto the back end of her car. Drew and Geoff would have their tents nearby.

Jenny, with her carry-all, followed Geoff to her own quarters. She was delighted with the two tiny canvas rooms under the one roof. In no time Geoff had opened other portable cases and suddenly there was unfolded a table for the kitchenette, a stool for the cook. There was also a washbasin, a tray, and even a rack over a squared plactic container for the dishes to dry in. He attached the camp oven to a wire and plug which in their turn were plugged in to the Land Cruiser's generator, a yard or two away at the back. In Jenny's sleeping room there was space for a camp stretcher, a stool, and—wonder of wonders—a mirror to hang from a cord attached to the centre pole.

While she had been ecstatically surveying her domain, Joey had laid quietly in the carton box. A blanket thrown over him partly kept in the warmth and partly prevented an escape.

Jenny went to work with a will in the kitchenette, unpacking smaller cartons of the prepared food that had been brought from Kalgoorlie. Geoff, after giving much advice about 'dust and clean up every day or you'll have Drew on your back,' took his departure to the forward part of his Land Rover. He heaved open the bonnet and started to do something with a piece of rag to the spark plugs.

Nicole came edgily round the now-connected Land Rover and tent house. She was taking all precautions against getting red dust or grease on her clothes.

"Oh! You *are* getting to work!" she said, poking her head into Jenny's confined world of camp oven and carton foods. "I was just checking. Everything has to be done by the clock from now on. There'll be no wish or whim. Sunup to sundown will be the rule of the day. Have you got the message, Jenny?"

"Oh yes!" Jenny said cheerfully, not looking round. "The oven works, and is actually getting hot. Hurrah for gadgetry! If someone would get the campfire going outside, we could have tea with dinner in half an hour."

"If *someone*—?" Nicole asked. *"You* are the some-one, Jenny. It's your job to get campfires going, as well as food warmed. This is not a picnic party."

"I'm sorry!" Jenny said. "All this is such fun I almost thought it *was* a picnic. If you'll just move aside, I'll be outward bound and make the fire—fire-sticks and all—in two shakes."

"A little more advice, Jenny. From now on we forget motels and town ways. This safari becomes an organized, and therefore regimented, expedition. Your schoolgirl way of talking just won't do. I should mention that fact of life to Geoff, too. He ought to know better by this time. He has been on safari before—" She broke off. A new thought had crossed her mind. "By the way," she said, "where is that wretched little animal?"

She looked round as if Joey were some wild beastie that needed to be driven off for safety's sake. For a split second Jenny all but forgot the new "order of the day" and almost said something sharp.

She thought again. No sense in getting on the wrong side of Nicole. All the same, Joey to her was not a "wretched little animal." Not to Drew, either.

"Joey," she said carefully, "is in the box by my bed. I'll take care— Oh, please, Nicole! *Please!* Don't move the lid. There's a crack left to let in enough air."

"By your *bed?*" Nicole asked, her fine eyebrows making even finer crescents above her eyes.

"Well—I could hardly put him in the kitchen, could I?" said Jenny. "I mean, he will mess. I know it's a 'he' because it's grey. If it were a 'she' it would be blue, wouldn't it? Like its mother. And we'd call it a doe?"

"Yes, all does are blue," Nicole said categorically. "And you can't possibly keep the thing by your bed. It's not healthy. The wild does—dingoes, as most people call them—frequently have ticks on them. It's just as likely that that animal is also infested."

"But it's not. Because I looked." Jenny tried to say this politely. Nicole stared at Jenny as if she were someone of nuisance value only.

Jenny wanted to hold her ground, but an instinct for safety reminded her Nicole was one of the bosses, and she herself was only the paid cook-rouseabout. She dropped her eyes and said quietly, "Please, Nicole. After all, it *was* Drew who found Joey and brought him back to the Cruiser. I'm sure he wouldn't want him to be thrown out in the cold."

There was a fractional minute of silence while Nicole digested this. Jenny felt mean enough to feel a tiny glow of triumph in her heart because she had used the right tack. Oh, the magic of Drew's name! It worked wonders.

"Very well. We'll see how it goes," Nicole said reluctantly. Then she added a last word before she went out: "But you'd better accept responsibility for it. Curiosity is built into the nature of those things, and in all probability it will try to get out in the night. They are night as well as day animals."

She turned and walked out. Jenny could hear her foam-soled safari shoes padding gently away, probably in the direction of Drew's tent-making.

Jenny turned back to her oven. She spat on her finger and touched the lid. It sizzled. She uncovered the small containers of prepared foods, slipped them in the oven, then cut down the battery power. Mustn't have them so hot the plastic melted, but just hot enough to be pleasantly edible. She found a carton of condiments and decided she would make a sauce that would surprise them all: a small tin of mushrooms mixed with a small tin of sweet corn, a teaspoon of packet tomato soup, a teaspoon of dried parsley—

It will be a sauce for kings, she thought. But her mental picture was not of crowned heads, but of Drew—and Geoff, too.

She popped her own head round the canvas flap that did for a door. She was trying to make up her mind which she dared do first—make that campfire or feed Joey again. If only Geoff would—

Her heart was suddenly all warm. No wonder she had thought of the men as she had winkled together that sauce! The campfire was smoking and about to leap into flame. And it was Geoff, with Drew standing by, who was making it.

The campfire dinner was over and everyone, even Nicole, had something pleasant to say about that sauce. As for the steaks, well—they were always good when fork-grilled over the coals, even though they had come out of their packets still half-frozen.

They sat around and talked. Geoff told anecdotes of his past safari with Drew while Drew maintained a studied silence that meant he was letting Geoff have his head, but only because it pleased him to do so. Nicole recounted some of the historical facts concerning the famous and now derelict Sons of Gwalia mine. She drew a map on the ground with a stick, showing Drew some of the side tracks they could take to bypass the main Kalgoorlie-Wiluna road.

"You have four station grills in all to cross," she said, very much the geographer." We have Barrett's permission to take the track between the inner and outer rings of water bores on Marandoo Station. Their sheep are out on the western boundaries at the moment. We could let the other stations know we're passing through over the two-way. That is, when the transceiver session comes on. They don't like strangers roaming their station properties; but so long as we let them know, they'll not raise difficulties."

Jenny had a funny but quite irrational feeling that Drew knew all about the track between Barrett's inner and outer rings of bores and was letting Nicole tell him to please Nicole. Which was absurd, of course. It had to be absurd, Jenny thought, because Nicole was the navigator. If Drew *knew*, then why have an official navigator at all? Unless it was just to have Nicole with him and to give her an important role.

Yet there was something more—some plan or future undertaking of which they did not speak. If Geoff knew about it, he was not speaking. Jenny had that curious left-out feeling again. Oh, well! It wasn't really her business, was it? And she was still an "unknown factor" to Drew and Nicole.

Jenny could not help but watch Drew as he sat crosslegged, his head bent as if intently studying those stick drawings. Every now and again he nodded as Nicole pointed out and named certain landmarks.

"Where's the black stump?" Jenny asked suddenly, then all but clapped her hand over her mouth. She'd been trying to be funny. And in this company, except for Geoff, it wasn't funny!

"There are black stumps everywhere," Nicole said severely. "You would have seen them all over ever since you left Yaraandoo."

"Beyond the black stump!" Drew said quietly, looking over the fire coals and into the darkness of the tree foliage. "It has a special meaning. It's come to signify the 'faraway land,' hasn't it? It's a kind of folklore expression."

" 'Forty miles east, then ten miles north. The water hole's five miles beyond the black stump!' " Geoff quoted, pleased with himself that he could quote anything. "Funny thing that, you know, Drew. Even today, with those old Outbackers the 'black stump's' always the *last* landmark that matters."

"So many of them," Jenny said a little sadly, forgetting her earlier mistake in trying to make a joke. "All those bushfires. But although the fires leave lots of stumps, there's always one that stands out as a sort of landmark. And maybe someone will need that particular landmark some day."

"And maybe survive because of it," Drew finished. "Which reminds me—that telephone box up there on the Pilbara, have you seen it, Nicole?"

She shook her head. "I thought they always used two-ways out there."

A two-way has been known to break down. That telephone box stands right out in the middle of nowhere. Nothing above spinifex-level in sight. A real nothing-land. With a sign that says: ninety-three miles to Salders. But the most important notice is the one that reads: 'Leave in good order. This telephone may save a life.' "

"But what if you didn't have the right money in your pockets?" Jenny queried, puzzled.

"You don't need money," Drew said. "It's free to the nearest town that has police, ambulance, Flying Doctor, etcetera. If we go up that way, Jenny, you could ring your mother at Yaraandoo from it. You'd have to reverse charges in that case."

There was quite a pause.

"It's rather wonderful," Jenny said at length. "That lonely red telephone box—I suppose it *is* red?"

"Very red. On a rise way outback on the spinifex plain," Drew added. "And no one has ever tampered with it, or left it in disorder."

Jenny gave a big sigh. "There's some good in human nature, after all!" she said.

Geoff threw a gum nut at her.

"Listen to our Jenny!" he said. "Not yet twenty and knows all about human nature! Disillusionment, too."

"Well, why not?" Nicole asked, being kind to the lower orders. "Youth is the time for lost illusions and sore hearts, isn't it, Jenny? Not to worry, child. I'm sure your John will be waiting for you when this safari is over. Meantime, Geoff seems to stand in ably."

Jenny wanted to look at Drew, but dared not. He was building coal castles in the fire with a long stick and was not looking up.

There was the smallest of small silences. Geoff broke it with a short laugh.

"Me? Who's made of nuts, bolts, steel, timber, and iron bridging the torrent of Jenny's affections? It would be pretty hard stuff to go to bed with, wouldn't it?"

"Would anyone like some more tea?" Drew asked, breaking up the conversation. "The billy's still half full. After that, it's time to turn in. All up, fed, and out by sunrise tomorrow. Right?"

It didn't work out that way. The dark held more than billy tea and sleep for the foursome in camp that night.

When the fire had been dampened down and each had said good night, Jenny went back to her own quarters, to find Joey half out of his box, his tail caught by the lid-hinge.

She was exasperated with herself for not thinking of it before. "A box is *not* a pouch for a baby." In a trice she had a whole spurt of brilliant ideas. First she would have to make a pouch. But with what? The canvas shoulder-bag she used for carrying her small things! Feed Joey, then put him in the bag, then hang up the bag. But where? The post on the outside that held the front corner of the tent upright! Hurrah! Joey, if he didn't sleep, would at least think he was watching the moonlight through the bush from his mother's pouch.

And it *was* moonlight. Beautiful clear silver light shone all over. It shone over the voiceless world of sand plain and red claypan, between the scattered mulga and spindly salmon gums. The night world was utterly silent. Nothing moved out there in the bush. Nothing stirred.

How lovely those pink trunks of the gum trees looked with the moonlight sheering past them, casting stilled shadows where it could not make a pool of silver light. It was wonderful.

When Joey was pouched up for the night, Jenny climbed between the unbleached cotton sheets on her camp stretcher. She lay on her back, looking out at the star-ridden sky, and listened to the silence.

How quickly Geoff had turned in and gone to bed? she wondered. Had he been tired after the long day? And why did *she* feel wide awake herself? Perhaps it had something to do with the incredible stillness, the white light through the trees, and the long, patterned shadows on the ground.

Her eyelids drooped. Funny, it wasn't noise that was keeping her awake. It was silence. How strange yet wonderful to hear absolutely nothing! Could one *hear* nothing? If not, then why did she find herself listening? And for what?

Then she knew. There were footsteps in that world of silver and silence.

She could hear them quite clearly now, though they were cautious and soft. There was the crackle of a dead stick, then the faint crunch of dead leaves. Something, someone, was abroad out there! Nicole and Drew coming back from a midnight walk? She had tried not to notice that when the campfire broke up, they had walked together into the trees on the far side of the track. There they had stood, talking in the shadows. Geoff had stamped out the fire, then walked in a foot-crashing way to his own tent.

"Call me if you find a snake on your feet in the night!" had been his last few jesting words to Jenny. "I'm in the pad next door. Even if it is ten feet away, I can make it in three jumps."

"I will," Jenny had promised. "Good night, kangaroo."

"And watch out for that baby one of your own. Any trouble at feeding time—I'll be there!"

Jenny had laughed, but underneath the laughter had been a wish that Geoff hadn't made that offer quite so loudly. She just hoped his voice wouldn't reach the other two—Nicole and Drew—under the shadow trees.

Then she had forgotten about them all.

Yet—in an unconscious sort of way—she had been listening for the footsteps of a man and woman coming back from the bush.

Now she could hear the steps, but from one person only. They were coming towards her tent, too.

Jenny watched the patch of moonlight outside. Beyond that patch were the slim black shadows of a mulga clump and a stand of salmon gums. Yet the steps, silenced by grass now, were not coming from that direction. They were coming from behind the tent, somewhere near the spot in which Nicole had parked her car and rigged up her own canvas cover.

If it *were* Nicole out and about, then she and Drew must have come back from their night walk a roundabout way and not have been so very long about it, after all. Perhaps they had just been discussing confidential business?

14

The steps were within a foot or two of her own tent opening now. And they had stopped.

Jenny felt positively spooky, which was silly. She wanted to laugh at herself. She also thought about calling out, but decided against it. It was not her business, in any event.

Joey's pouch hanging from the tent's upright was no more than a half-moon shadow that broke the straight lines of the doorway.

It moved. Slowly it swayed to the left and out of sight.

There was an indeterminate sound, then a small thump, as of something dropping to the ground. The pouch shadow swung back into line, no longer a moon-shaped bulge. It was now flat—and empty?

Jenny threw back the top sheet and jumped out of bed.

"Joey!" she cried. "He's out!"

Her shortie pyjamas were a sufficiently respectable cover, but she didn't even think of it. She ran through the opening out into the moonlit world. She could have read a book by that light, but she didn't think about that, either. She concentrated on one thing—a small, hopping creature dark against the white-lit ground, moving as fast as it could into the shadows of the black-stemmed trees.

"Joey! Joey!" she cried as she raced after it. "Joey! Come back!" Yet she knew he would not hear, and even if he did he would not come. He was not trained. He wouldn't know that she wanted to save him, not

116

harm him. The small animal hopped on and on at a great pace across the shadowed ground—up one slight slope and down another, into a clearing. Jenny ran after him, not even noticing the dried-out ground sticks and small, sharp gibber stones biting into her feet.

Across the clearing the small shadow hopped, round a clump of trees and some low bush, and into another circular clearing.

Right in the centre of that clearing was the rounded, inverted-saucer shape of a mullock heap.

Jenny did not stop to ask herself if this was a shaft or an old throw-away tip from some small spec mine. She continued to run. Joey hopped on and disappeared over the rim of the heap. Jenny ran up the slope—only a yard or two—scrabbling her feet amongst the white and pink quartz rubble.

As she went over the top she realized it *was* a shaft. But it was too late to stop. She was slithering on the down side just as Joey tried to leap the hole. But he was too small and too young to make it. His tail and hind paws slipped backwards. He writhed around, then was suddenly gone, down into the shaft.

Jenny's feet crumbled under her. She was sliding on her backside, the loose rubble of small stones carrying her with them. Instinctively one hand flew out to catch an old ant-eaten post that had once held the miner's bucketwheel. It broke. A foot of the old, weather-worn timber piece came off in her hand. She, too, went down the hole.

It was perhaps ten feet, no more. And at the bottom there was water, old water, slimed with moss, and moreover with something squirming in it—some living creature other than Joey.

As she stood on the mud ground she was up to her knees in the water. But she managed to grasp Joey by his tail as he tried the impossible jump to the surface.

"Little beastie," she said, all but crying. "Dear Heaven! What do we do now?" She looked upwards to the dark, star-spattered sky above her.

A white dust of cloud with a silver lining meant the

moon was somewhere behind it. In another minute the
cloud would move on and the moon would shed its
light straight down into the shaft. She knew all this and
actually thought about it while she tied Joey inside her
pyjama coat. She could actually feel him clawing at her
chest and neck with a pair of small but strong hind
legs. She could see and hear the slide of the pink and
white stones scattering down in the aftermath of her
own fall.

The water felt horrible around her legs. And the
"something" continued to slither against the old
wooden planks that had once shored up the shaft.

The white pin-cushion cloud fluffed on and then the
moon shone down on her upturned face like a white
torchlight, pointing through the mouth of the shaft
above. She could clearly see the dank, weathered timbers lining the shaft.

"Oh, please, Moon, stay there so that I can see how
to climb out!"

She smacked Joey hard with the flat of her hand to
make him keep still. Amazingly, he did just that. Do
kangaroos, like cats, smack their young? she wondered,
without actually realizing she was capable even at this
moment of wondering about something. Her eyes ran
down from the top part of the old timbers to the water-
line at the bottom of the well now scrabbling round her
legs. She was trying to spot a foothold she might take,
if the moon would only stay there long enough.

She had reached a point of desperation in the depths
of her being when she saw what it was that slithered.
Not a snake, thank God! It was a goanna, and it was
pointing its diamond head upwards as if it too searched
for a foothold in the timbers. Jenny saw that it was all
bone, with tight skin drawn over its skeleton. She was
torn between pity and despair.

"It's been down here a long time," she said aloud,
smacking Joey again. This second smack was even
more effective than the first had been, for Joey was
now comforted by his new pouch made of Jenny's
warm flesh on one side and the tight pull of her pyjama

coat on the other side. "It's starving, poor little thing," she said of the goanna, talking both to herself and (for comfort's sake) to Joey, too. "It hasn't been able to climb those timbers, and it's a climber. It has long, curled nails on its feet and can climb trees."

She leaned back against the wall and closed her eyes.

If a goanna can't get out, she thought, I'll never make it. That is to say, *we'll* never make it, Joey. How long before they find I'm missing? Not till morning. Is either Geoff or Drew a tracker?

She looked up again, then closed her eyes and began a prayer of thanks. A head had appeared in the opening above. It was almost blocking out the moon. Her prayer hadn't actually put itself into words before she heard a voice, *his* voice—Drew's voice.

"Jenny? What the devil are you doing down that shaft? You little—"

"Don't say it," she called back, and wiped the back of her spare hand across her eyes. She wasn't crying, of course. It was just that her eyes were watering. "I know all the things I am, but I had to get Joey. He ran away."

"Hell and damnation!" was Drew's immediate reply. He withdrew his head, which seemed to Jenny as if he were withdrawing his pleasure too, for ever and ever.

Then she could hear his voice cutting the air above like a sharp whip-crack.

"Over here, Geoff! Right! I'll take the bigger torch. Get a coil of rope. Make it double fast. That air down there can be undiluted poison."

His head came back into the opening.

"Jenny, are you all right?"

"Yes. So's Joey. He's not scrabbling about so much in my pyjamas now. I think he feels comfortable."

"Listen, girl!" Drew's voice had a note of controlled anger and exasperation in it. It was almost a pleasure to Jenny to see that *something* could move him. "Forget about that damned animal," he said. "We have to get you out of there before you die of poisoning or something."

"I'm not cut."

"It's what you're *breathing* that matters," he said flatly. "Now listen and listen hard. If there's any step or higher elevation you can get your feet on, then stay on it. Keep your head up as high as you can."

"It's all right, Drew. The air's not poisoned down here. It's quite all right."

"How in a devil's circus would *you* know?" His voice had a certain fury in it now. "Carbon monoxide has no smell and sulphur dioxide very little."

"It's nothing to do with *smell*," Jenny called up. She was getting a crick in her neck now; so she took a moment off to look down instead of up. The goanna was limp, in the late stages of exhaustion—but still trying to get a purchase with its feet on the steep vertical timbers.

"I know because of the goanna," she explained, painfully tilting her head up again. "It's been here ages and it's not poisoned. Well, not yet, anyway."

"Goanna be—" Drew began. Then he broke off.

What he'd been going to say was evidently not fit for ears either above or below ground level.

"I'm not frightened at all—at least, not since I saw you up there," Jenny called, as if *he* were the one who needed reassuring. "I'm quite comfortable—except, that is, for the rather nasty water. It's sort of thick. But Joey's lying still. My pyjama coat and me make a nice warm pouch for him."

The head and shoulders came right into the hole now.

"Jenny, will you save your breath! Don't talk again till I tell you you can. Don't breathe in deeply. Shallow breathing—"

"But the goanna is still alive—" she began to explain once more. But Drew had disappeared from sight. She was talking to the air and to a silver-lit sky with its bevy of twinkling stars. The moon had moved on, or was it the earth that had moved? Oh well, a bit of both! Anyhow the moon was gone, and so was Drew's head. But it was only a temporary disappearance. Fifteen seconds later not one, but *two* heads appeared, they were outlined by the sky, which was still lit by the passing moon.

"Geoff!" She could hardly get it out. There were tears very near. Geoff had come! She'd be all right now. It was something about Yaraandoo people sticking together.

"Jenny, you pest of a girl," Geoff's voice was saying, "what the hell are you doing down there?"

"Keeping company with a menagerie," she called past a lump in her throat. "I've a baby kangaroo and a goanna for company."

"Drown them both," he shouted, pretending wrath. "What a bother to have to fuss with you at this late hour! How in the name of fortune did your parents let you out of domestic custody? Hang on a minute. Drew's coming down with the rope."

His head disappeared and there were sounds of male voices talking from somewhere above. A looped rope was being lowered.

Geoff's head came back.

"Slip that loop over your head and under your arms, then tighten it, but—*please*—don't put it round your neck and choke yourself."

"I won't, but I'll have to take care it doesn't choke Joey, looped under my arms. And John doesn't have an 'o' on the end of his name, and my mount's name is Redcoat, and he's a gelding, not a horse." She was getting her own back from a safe distance.

Then she broke off. Geoff's head had disappeared and another one had appeared on the further side of the hole.

"Are you roped up, Jenny?" Drew asked, flatly calm. He was concealing anger, Jenny thought.

"Yes. It'll be a bit hard to keep Joey safe."

"Of that I'm sure," his voice said steadily, but she sensed he was still angry. Or was he? "I'll tighten the rope from this end and Geoff will rope up to a rock up here. Tight enough now? Keep your arms down by your sides. If you raise them and the rope loosens, it could slip over your head."

"Excuse me, but of course my arms are down," Jenny said. "I have to hold my menagerie."

"Your what?"

But the head was gone; so he wasn't waiting for an answer. Jenny decided she had to be very docile and good from this minute on. Drew's voice had been loaded with undercurrents she couldn't quite identify. But it was he who had saved Joey before. He wouldn't—well, he couldn't— Or could he?

A pair of long legs were descending into the shaft. Jenny squeezed back against the wall. Inch by inch the legs became a torso. Then, face to face with her, was a man's head. It was Drew.

"I hope your feet won't go in that water with a splash," she said hopefully. They didn't. Geoff, who was doing the lowering from up above, knew his job.

Drew, too, was now knee-deep in water.

So now there's two of us, Jenny thought. But she didn't dare say it aloud. What expression she could see on Drew's face was much too serious for whatever frivolity survived in her mind. It had been there ever since she'd finished that nasty slide and found herself more or less unharmed, although standing in a mess of slime.

She thought perhaps Drew was really very angry. Was it because she had run after Joey? Or was it because she'd been acting—well, sort of as if it were all an adventure good for laughs at some later date?

"Oh dear!" She looked down at the bundle attached to her by her pyjama coat. She had the lower front edges of the coat gathered together and tied securely in a good, stout reef knot. She was rather proud of that reef knot—right over left, then left over right.

She hoped Drew would notice it and know she was past the age of granny knots.

But he wasn't looking at her handiwork. He'd taken the torch out of his own pyjama pocket and was flashing it round the walls of the shaft, then upwards; he was searching for footholds in the rotting timbers, just as she had done.

He brought the torchlight back to her face.

"Are you all right, Jenny?" he asked.

"Of course," she said. "A few scratches. Maybe a bruise or two in the morning." She did not mention her backside, which was now beginning to declare itself painfully. It was thoroughly scratched, and probably also bruised.

Geoff's head appeared again, silhouetted in the hole above.

"Say when you're ready, Drew," he called. "We have got both ends slip-roped up here now. Send Jenny up first. Then you gather in the slack as she comes."

"Ready, Jenny?" Drew asked, flashing the torchlight in her face again.

"Yes. I know how you're doing it. A bit like a flying fox, except it's vertical instead of horizontal."

"Exactly. Now, ready?"

"No-o-o. Please—I want the goanna, too. *Please, Drew.*" He was using the light end of the torch to make an examination of her general condition; so she couldn't really see the expression on his face. But she knew it was dead-pan cold.

"The blasted goanna?"

"Yes. It wants to be saved, too. It's been trying and trying long before I came. It's so weak—"

"You've got the joey safely cradled up? Now stand still while I test that the loop is tightened up for safety."

He tightened her rope through the slip-knot, not looking her in the eyes even once, although they stood there face to face. His iron-strong hands dealt with the hauser-type rope in a professional manner.

"The goanna—please, Drew," she said steadily, trying to look at him so that his eyes would meet hers.

He tested the rope once again by running two fingers round the inside of it where it met her body. Jenny drew in her breath so as not to embarrass him. Then she realized she should have expelled it, so as to make herself slimmer.

"You put on two inches then," he said in a studied and noncommittal way.

"I'll diet as of now," she said contritely. Drew tested the firmness of the loop yet again. He looked up skywards.

"Right, Geoff!" he called. "Haul away."

"The *goanna!*" There were nearly tears in her voice. Then their eyes *did* meet—in that artificial gloaming.

He put out his hand and touched the side of her head.

"I'll bring it up, Jenny," he said. There was a sudden gentleness in his voice.

"Thank you," she said, in a muffled whisper.

The rope was already tightening. Suddenly she and Drew were in action. He lifted her up vertically out of the water, almost as if he were hoisting her in the air. His hands were like two iron plates on either side of her waist. The rope tautened and gradually, second by second, it took its purchase on her. Drew's hands eased.

"Use your feet, one after the other—as for walking—against the wall," Drew commanded. "Imagine you're walking up the timbers. Keep as straight as you can so that you don't hit the wall behind you with your back. That's right!"

Then with a shout to Geoff: "She's coming up, clear and simple."

It was only minutes later that her head and shoulders were through the hole.

Geoff was lying prone, curved over the mullock, his arms outstretched towards her. Then he caught her under the armpits and pulled. As she came out Geoff slithered backwards, drawing her with him. Suddenly she was standing on the lip of the mound and Geoff was scrambling to his feet, holding her arm with one hand tightly, as if he might never let it go.

Jenny gulped. "Oh Geoff!" she said, almost near tears.

"Right away with the rope, Nicole," he called over his shoulder. There seemed to be a lump in his throat. Then he turned again to Jenny.

"You hurt any?" His voice was still uneven.

Was Geoff angry with her, too?"

"I'm perfectly all right," Jenny said with what dignity she could muster. She couldn't bear Geoff's anger, too. Her feet and legs felt sticky, as if they'd been in some kind of warm treacle.

"Ugh! It's awful down there," she said.

"You ought to know. You went," Geoff said bluntly. "Now you're saved, just step out of the way, will you, Pesty? We have to bring Drew up. Remember? He went down there after you."

"Yes—I'm sorry." Jenny needed Geoff's help to loosen the rope and to slip it over her shoulders and head.

"So Nicole's on the winch, is she? Is there anything Nicole can't do?" she asked.

Geoff was tautening Drew's rope and not looking at her. The moonlight was so bright he probably could see she was all right. But he was silent. Somehow Jenny felt sad at the loss of Geoff's conspiratorial friendship. Her confidence wavered for the first time. She was now thinking of what Nicole would say.

All the same, when this safari ended, she might just ask Nicole how a joey could possibly be tipped out of its satchel in the middle of the night?

It couldn't have been anyone else but Nicole, could it? Nicole hadn't liked the joey. She'd disapproved of Jenny having it near her sleeping quarters. And she had been up and about—fully dressed.

It had not been Geoff, and it had not been Drew. Of that Jenny was sure. It had not been the joey himself, either. Or could it have been? Would he have been old enough to jump out of his mother's pouch?

But—there'd been those footsteps. That soft slipper-soled tread over the dried sticks and fallen leaves. If not Nicole's, then whose?

Geoff was now talking down the shaft. This time it was he who was giving the orders.

"Three twitches as a signal, Drew. And we'll haul away."

"I'll hold that wretched little creature." It was Nicole coming out of the moon-struck shadows. "Heavens above, Jenny, your legs look a sight! You'd better get the camp shower going. But don't waste the water; we'll all want a shower in the morning."

Jenny hugged the baby kangaroo.

"No, thank you. I'll hold Joey," she said, warding off Nicole with one hand. She was afraid Nicole would let the little creature go. It could be lost in the bush, or even fall down that beastly shaft again.

Nicole seemed surprised at Jenny's sudden protective move.

"Well, please yourself,'" she said. "Heavens, girl, what are those stains on your pyjama coat?"

Jenny did not tell her they were possibly—probably—blood stains from Joey's claws.

"Everything's dirty—down there," she said defensively. "Yes, I'll go and have a shower; but not till Drew's up and out. He could slip."

In the pale moon-gloaming light, Jenny could see the superior smile on Nicole's face.

"Drew will climb out of that, with or without the help of Geoff's rope," Nicole said calmly. "There's nothing helpless about Drew in any situation."

Jenny wanted to say, "Well, you ought to know!" But she remembered in time that harmony is a must on any safari.

There came a concatenation of noises from the shaft. Geoff was doing something with the rope and Drew was heaving himself from the shaft mouth. His hands were pressing hard on a timbered cross-piece. His arms straightened themselves like a weightlifter's; then he was up and out.

"Poor dear!" Nicole said casually. "Just look at your

feet and legs! For heaven's sake, what have you bundled in your pyjama top, Drew?"

"One claw-footed lizard—a half-starved, half-drowned goanna."

"My goodness!" Nicole exclaimed. "Are we thinking of setting up a zoo on the back trailer? And why a goanna?"

"I don't know. Ask Jenny." Drew pulled out the almost inert creature. "Here, Geoff," he said, "you look after this one. I'm sure it will take all Jenny's time cleaning up that joey." He threw the small reptile to Geoff. Geoff caught it neatly.

"Anyone have any flies?" Geoff asked of the air. "This thing needs feeding. It's probably been down there some time. All bones."

"I dare say Jenny can and will rustle up something," Drew said dryly, buttoning up his pyjama coat. "Meantime I need the powerful torch and ten minutes."

"For what?" asked Geoff in a strained voice. He was trying to prevent the goanna from slithering out of his hands, and at the same time hold its small diamond head in a position from which it could not bite a finger or thumb.

"Oh Drew, you are in a mess!" Nicole began again, very solicitous now.

Drew's state of mess, Jenny thought, was a matter of concern to Nicole. Her own appearance had just been something distasteful.

"Well, that's as it may be," Drew said. "I've other things to think about now. Jenny? Do something about those representatives of the animal world, will you? Then clean up and put yourself to bed. That is, if you are feeling okay: Any damage anywhere?"

Cuts and bruises, Jenny thought. But she did not say so aloud. She wasn't going to get any sympathy, that was for sure.

"I'm all right," she answered. "Let me put Joey in the pouch, Geoff. Then I'll nip back and take the goanna."

"Absolutely not," Geoff said. "I know the right place

for this thing. A good ant-trail in the bush. It will look after itself. Here goes!"

He took six long strides to the edge of the bush and set the goanna down. To Jenny's amazement the little reptile took itself off at top speed. In a matter of seconds, it had disappeared.

"Bit it was so weak——"

"Didn't like the water, that's all," Geoff said. "One smell of the bush and it has conjured up the strength to survive. Right, Nicole? You're the ecologist."

"Right. And the same goes for the wretched little kangaroo," Nicole said. "In the bush it will find its own way to survive. In case you didn't know, Jenny, that's why the mother throws it out of her pouch when she's in danger. She's giving it a better than one chance in two to survive on its own resources."

Jenny half turned, as if to go back to her quarters. She was hugging the joey tighter than ever. Then she looked back at Nicole. The moonlight swept the whole area with a silver light, and she could see every detail of all that was around her.

"Did *you*——? I mean, did you *see* who tipped the joey out of its pouch?" she asked quietly.

"Did I——*what*?"

For a broken moment, Jenny gave Nicole credit for good acting. Drew and Geoff were coiling up the rope. Now Drew straightened up and turned around.

"That is why I want the power torch," he said. "I think we had a visitor at the camp site tonight. I'll check for tracks."

"You think——it was the same as——?" Geoff began, straightening up himself.

"I don't think anything until I check," Drew said flatly. "Nicole? You and Jenny go back to camp, will you? And, Nicole, I think Jenny might need some medical attention."

"*Me*—medical?——" Jenny blurted out.

"Yes, *you*. Those scratches. Nicole? You'll check her over, will you? We don't want a blood-poisoning case on our hands."

"Blood-poisoning?" Jenny was trying not to be surprised, let alone indignant.

"Yes. That slime down the shaft—the small 'roo had been in it, too."

Jenny wilted.

"Oh! For goodness sake! Well, I suppose I'd better—"

"You had. And Nicole will supervise. By the way, Nicole, have you any iodine in the medical kit? It stings and Mercurochrome doesn't." He paused and added, "Some people, who shall be nameless, *deserve* iodine. It's more effective, anyway."

Geoff gave a guffaw of laughter.

"The punishment fits the crime, Jenny," he said. "The Big Boss Fella goes in for torture of those of his slaves who break the rules and fall down mine shafts."

Jenny indulged in a moment of justified self-pity. She'd run to save a small animal, had fallen down a shaft, and gotten herself a load of bruises. All Joey had done in return was scratch her. All Drew was doing now was recommending something that stung. All Geoff was doing was hooting with laughter. And all Nicole was about to do was administer a punitive medicine!

Jenny almost wanted to send Joey scuttling into the bush after the goanna. Nobody seemed to recognize that she had been out saving two lives tonight. Well, one and a half—after all, Drew *had* brought up the goanna, though much against his will.

"Come along, Jenny," Nicole said, and tapped her arm. "Let the men go moonlight-tracking while you and I seek the shower and the medical chest."

"What or whom are they tracking?" Jenny asked, bewildered. She was also trying to shake off her feeling of gloom.

"They'll tell us when they get in, in the morning. Till then, we just have to wait and wonder, don't we?" Her tone of voice was soothing, perhaps even mollifying. It occurred to Jenny that, give Nicole an important job to do and she became a different person. She was even being pleasant and friendly now, not critical—as well she might have been.

And yet—and yet—! Why did she think at the back of her mind that it was Nicole who had let Joey out of his pouch? Those footsteps! Had they been too soft and too light for a man's tread? Well, not altogether.

For the first time Jenny realized she had not noticed what either Geoff or Drew had been wearing on their feet. It had been dark in the shaft when Drew came down and, of course, his feet had been immediately immersed in that green algae-water. He would have shaken off his shoes!

She tried to call to mind an accurate picture of Geoff coiling the rope into a neat nest after she'd been hauled up. It had been bright moonlight—so bright she could have read a book by it. Yet she had not noticed Geoff's feet.

She glanced down at Nicole's footwear. Yes, they were those foam-soled safari shoes which Nicole always wore. They would be soft enough—that is, if Nicole walked carefully, which she was not doing now. Dried leaves and tiny fallen sticks were cracking away cheerfully under her feet as they walked back to the camp.

And strangely, when they reached Jenny's quarters, Nicole helped her to bathe her chest scratches with kind, gentle care and attention. She put Mercurochrome on them, not the iodine that heartless Drew had suggested. She actually became motherly—a complete change of role—even standing patiently by while Jenny fed Joey and then carefully packed him back in the pouch.

"I don't feel like leaving him, in case—" Jenny began doubtfully.

"Pull the zip further along," advised Nicole. "He'll get plenty of air if you leave even two inches. And air can get in where the sides have been laced, too."

"Yes, of course." Jenny could not make herself believe that Nicole could be as deceptive as this. It just didn't add up.

But if Nicole was innocent, then who *had* let Joey

out? Someone had done it. Jenny had seen the pouch being drawn back, had heard the thump, had seen the flattened pouch fall back into place—an empty canvas bag with laced sides and a zip top.

"Nicole," she said suddenly, as she came out of the small canvas shower, "who do you think let Joey out?" Best to ask and be done with it.

Nicole finished her ministrations and turned away. She reached in her jacket pocket for cigarettes and a box of matches. Jenny did not take her eyes from Nicole's face, although the tent was lighted only by the pale yellow glow of a storm lantern.

Nicole looked over a lighted match at Jenny.

"Who says anyone *let* him out? Are you sure he didn't just *get* out?" Her voice was quite steady.

"Yes," Jenny said simply. "I heard footsteps. They stopped. Then the pouch moved, and Joey fell out with a thump."

"And you ran out after him immediately?"

"Like a flash."

"You must have seen someone then, surely? That is, if there was anyone." Nicole's eyes were interrogating. There was in them a will to discover what Jenny knew, if anything.

It was Jenny who looked away first.

"I could hear Joey jumping, after he was out. So I looked at *him*—at Joey, I mean. I could see his shadow moving in and out of the moonlight patches; so I ran after him."

"You saw no one else?"

"No-o," Jenny said slowly. "I saw no one."

Nicole shook ash from her cigarette. She looked back at Jenny sharply, almost as if to catch Jenny out.

"You told Drew this?"

"Well—not in detail. I can't remember exactly what I did say, except that—"

Nicole's manner changed back to her habitually brisk and authoritative one.

"Then get to sleep and forget about it. I'll tell Drew

about it when he comes in. Or, if it's too late then, in the morning."

Jenny shook out the top sheet on her camp stretcher and went to bed.

15

Jenny could not get comfortable. The heat seemed hotter—if there was such a way of putting it. (She was too tired to think in good English.) She was actually too tired to sleep. Her legs were stinging from the midgies that had bitten her down in that slimy water at the bottom of the shaft.

It had been a no-go try, that shaft! Some fossiker of long ago had dug a hole and kept on digging, hoping upon hope that any minute his spade would strike something good. Pay dirt, they called gold specks in those days. He—that fossiker of long ago—must have thought it was worth his while, or he wouldn't have gone so deep or have timbered up the sides.

Jenny lay on her bed alternately rubbing one leg against the other, according to which was stinging more at any given moment. She found herself wondering why Drew had gone off—at this hour of night, too! Was he in search of whoever had turned Joey out of his pouch? Because someone *did* turn Joey out.

Another unhappy thought entered her mind. Suppose Drew didn't believe her! Suppose he thought that she, Jenny, had not described the facts quite as they had actually happened!

Who was he looking for right out there along the verges of the bush! And Geoff might be with him, too! Now, if only Geoff would come back—

Jenny's eyelids drooped over her eyes. Sleep was almost upon her. Then they flew open again.

When a few moments ago she had thought of Drew

searching in the shadows of the bush, she had had a mental picture of him.

That suddenly had gone, and it was no longer the image of Drew which was imprinted in her mind. It was the medium-sized figure of a man—neither short nor tall, neither fat nor thin, but something in between.

He was the man she had seen in the early morning, before sunrise, standing in the shadows of the bush fringe along the path to the roadhouse kitchen. He had had dark eyes, she was sure; yet somehow some light from somewhere—perhaps the light reflected from something he held in his hand, palm up—had caught him so that his eyes seemed to shine. And he had had on a cotton hat. It was like the narrow-brimmed cotton hats the truckies wore, although theirs were brown or jungle green, inevitably dusty, and sometimes downright dirty. But this man—the one in the bushes—had worn a *white* cotton hat, and it had been *clean*. It had had to be clean, or Jenny would not have been able to see so clearly in the no-light of early dawn. The brim had been turned down all round. That was the way he wore it, and that was why Jenny had known it was white. Otherwise it wouldn't have shown up so clearly in the shadows of the trees and bushes, would it?

Jenny wasn't a farm girl for nothing. On farms and cattle stations and sheep-runs, you learned when you were ever so young to notice anything that was different. You noticed, for instance, when the sheep were walking heads down, and away from the water. You would know, then that something was wrong. Perhaps Bret, the musterer, had forgotten to turn on the water-cocks along the boundary and the bores out there had nothing to give to the sizzling hot troughs. If that were so, the sheep, dried-out inside as well as outside, and still heavy with their wool because it was a week or two from shearing time, would die from heat stroke and thirst.

So you would go out there to check, and this time the sheep *wouldn't* die—thanks to the fact that you had noticed something different about them—

Jenny's thoughts rambled on. By this time, she was edging near sleep again. She had to force herself to put a full stop to the memories of things that could happen if one weren't a noticing sort of person.

Then her eyes flew open again. Her neck was stiff now, but she managed to shake her head, and so shake off sleep for another few minutes.

She needed to go back in her mind, to remember something that she had noticed about that man in the bush by the roadhouse. He had been the *only* man or boy she had seen since she had come into the eastern areas who wore a new, clean white hat. And that mattered in the Outback. You needed to know about someone who was different. And when it was a stranger, everyone else round and about had to know about him, too. Who was he? And what was his business? It was the custom of the land—and was as firm as law—to identify anyone out-of-the-ordinary.

Jenny pushed her feet against the end of the stretcher bed and sat up. Should she tell Drew? Well, she could hardly go out looking for him in the dark. She was already in disgrace.

Nicole? Nicole was no go! She wasn't—exactly—approachable. Also she would probably say, as well as think, that Jenny was a little mad. Jenny wasn't sure herself that she wasn't a little mad. Yet whether she was a laughing stock or not, she had to report to someone. It was a little late to be doing it, of course; but it had to be done—specially as tonight the camp had had an odd visitor of sorts! (Witness her own stiff neck, stiff back, stiff arms, and stinging legs!)

Jenny pushed her feet into rubber thongs and pulled a blouse and shorts on over her shortie pyjamas. She knew the basic essence of her thinking made sense.

She had not heard Drew come back from his search. She could not tell Nicole. So she would have to tell Geoff. This gave her a feeling of comfort.

She stole her way out of the tent, touching Joey's pouch gently just to make sure he was still there, then starting off very soft-soled to where Geoff ought to be sleeping. But he wasn't there.

Jenny was nonplussed. He hadn't gone trailing with Drew. But perhaps he had gone later, which would mean he had known where Drew was heading. And how could that be?

He couldn't possibly be visiting Nicole in her tent at this hour—or any hour—Jenny felt positively sick at the awfulness of such a thing. Not Geoff! Oh, please not *Geoff!*

But if he was, what did it matter?

It *did* matter. For the life of her, Jenny couldn't think why it should give her such a sharp pain in the chest; yet it certainly did! Nicole couldn't have *everyone*—Drew, Pete the Prospector, and now Geoff. That really hurt.

Jenny went back to her own tent, put herself to bed again, and with deliberate restraint prevented herself from becoming watery round the eyes. Oh, well—! Soreness in her body, weariness in her muscles, and a feeling of belonging to no one—it was all just too much for her.

She let Nature take over, and within minutes was deeply asleep.

Their camp was late in stirring next morning. On waking, Jenny fed Joey first because the silence outside as the light came slowly over the land from the east told her that none of the others was up and about yet.

Joey's meal finished, his pouch-pocket cleaned and himself put back in it again, Jenny went about making a campfire. Breakfast was much nicer and more fun around a campfire than around that modern invention, the battery-run camp oven, with all its fittings and tricky devices.

Nicole was the first one into the canvas shower rigged up under one of the trees. It wasn't the sort of morning when a greeting was in order. They both omitted it. Nicole nodded her head and yawned. Jenny nodded her head and poked another stick into the fire under the billy.

She sat squatting on her heels like a real Outbacker until Drew, and then Geoff, had followed in Nicole's train and had themselves fresh buckets of water hung to the tree branches behind the canvas screen. You tipped this water over yourself with a pull-rope. It was the heavenliest sort of shower, if you liked cold water—!

Nobody as yet had spoken to Jenny. Even Geoff had only yawned, then scratched his head, as he looked at her. She was now boiling the billy. At the same time, she was raking together a heap of glowing coals on which she would presently place lamb chops, retrieved from the portable cooler.

At last, all washed and dressed, the other three sat down round the fire. They drank tea from large aluminum mugs and eyed the mounting pile of lamb chops. Jenny was working with a long wire fork. First she turned the chops, then speared them and put them on a stand of hot stones.

Geoff was the first to speak.

"So how is Joey this morning?" he asked.

Jenny pretended grumpiness. "Very well, thank you. Taking his food, and keeping warm in his pouch, I hope."

"Are we talking about an invalid?" Nicole asked coldly.

Jenny did not answer; she was momentarily overwhelmed by a show of thoughtfulness—even kindness—from Drew. He took her long fork from her, speared two lamb chops, one after the other, onto a plate, and set it, together with knife and fork, before her.

"Have some breakfast, Jenny," he said. "When you've finished that—and the slice of toast Geoff will no doubt make for you—we'll talk. Yes?"

"Yes. Thank you. I mean, thank you for the chops."

Then, horror of horrors, she found herself blushing—in such an unmistakable way that she knew it could not be missed by anyone. And all because Drew had waited on her! She immediately tucked a choice cut of lamb into her mouth before she could say anything worse.

Breakfast was soon over. While Jenny set up the large aluminum wash-up bowl to balance on two rocks, the other three moved off into the shade of thin-leafed mulga and fell into conference attitudes.

Talking business! Jenny poured boiling water from the two billy cans into the bowl. Hers was the job to wash up, and theirs the job to discuss the day's work.

Drew struck a match for Nicole's cigarette and then for his own. Geoff put his foot on their dead match, then took out more matches and lit his own cigarette.

To Jenny, looking at them through veils of steam, it seemed that Drew and Nicole were doing all the talking. Geoff was merely listening. She wished very much that she had been experienced enough to have taken part in those planning talks. All sorts of exciting things might begin to happen now, and she longed to be equal and with-it all the way.

The camp had been fixed down in a near permanent way, and all the stores had been unloaded. The parts of a largish box-cupboard had been fitted together, and it was now Jenny's job to cache away the stores as methodically as possible in the limited space.

She thought of the three of them over there as the "Council of Equals." A good name, too, she thought. Twice she saw Geoff shake his head, then immediately look across the space of dry grass and camp embers towards herself. Were they talking about her? And if so, why? Geoff at one stage must have put in something fairly tough-worded. Jenny could see this by his expression.

What were they saying? She wished she knew. Were they still angry because of last night's events? She would just have to work harder and quicker, make herself indispensable, and then maybe they'd forget—or at least forgive her for taking to her heels after Joey last night and, even worse, slipping down a mine shaft! Well, that last had been the unforgivable part, she supposed. She didn't think Drew would have been against her taking off to Joey's rescue. What he had minded was that she had slipped down the shaft. He had already given her plenty of warning about being careful of old, disused mine shafts.

Jenny went on putting things away. Every now and again, she would surreptitiously glance towards the threesome. Would Drew be telling them what he had found last night when he'd gone off on his tracking tour? Why hadn't he done it before breakfast, so that she too might feel included?

She had just reached the point of taking herself to task for feeling "left out" again, when she saw Geoff break away from the group and come loping cheerfully towards the camp site.

"So what goes?" she asked, averting her gaze to check that the last of the fire embers were dead and cold.

"Drew and Nicole are taking off for distant places. For the day, anyway," he said.

"You, too?"

"Well—yes and no to that. I've a job to finish hereabouts, and then—maybe later—"

Jenny adopted her stout and sturdy stance.

"Geoff," she said, "I hope you are not dreaming of staying here in case I don't like being left alone, or something old-fashioned like that!"

"Well," he said ruminating, "it's not exactly *you* we're thinking about."

"Oh, no?"

He lit another cigarette and took a long time to kill the match very dead by burying it in the sand with the heel of his boot.

"Geoff, you *are* aggravating! Please tell me what goes?"

"Hah! The right cue," he said. "What *goes*. Goes is the definitive word." Through the cigarette smoke she could see he was again wearing his old teasing smile. "A kangaroo hops, a lizard slithers, a bird flies, but a car goes. A nice big car, that has radial tyres with a diamond pattern to them. Now if you noticed Nicole's beautiful Mercedes at all, you will have seen that it, too, has radial tyres. But not with a diamond pattern. Hers are ladder-patterned—"

Jenny all but stamped her foot. "Geoff, *please!* Will you stop fooling? You've—" Her voice petered out and there were very nearly tears at the back of her eyes. He threw his cigarette into the dead fire-coals and came over to her. He slid his arm along her shoulder.

"I'm sorry, Jenny," he said. "I didn't think you minded being left out. It's Drew's way of doing things. It *is* his business, you know."

Jenny blinked her eyes. "I'm the one who's sorry," she said. "It was just that I *was* feeling left out. I had no right, of course."

He gave her shoulder a squeeze, then quickly let go.

"Stand still! Don't move either foot." he commanded.

Jenny was too much of a farm girl not to know what that order—together with the tone of voice—meant. She stood statue-still. Geoff bent down, picked up something in his hand, gave it a sharp flick with his wrist, then let it fly through the air into a nest of bushes.

"Only a sand snake," he said cheerfully.

He buried both his hands in his pockets and sat down on the stump they'd been using as a breakfast table.

"That grid-iron we passed over yesterday was the south boundary of Nat Barrett's place," he said. "We didn't close in on the homestead—roughly four miles away—because we didn't want to be a burden on their home and kitchen. Got it?"

"Yes." Jenny was puzzled. "But I thought they were partners or something. The papers they were signing back at the motel—"

"Well, they're partners of a kind; but they don't want the whole Outback to know it."

"Was it Nat Barrett's radial-tyre mark you meant?"

"It's what Drew thought possible though not probable. So he went out last night to eliminate Nat's tyre marks from consideration. He knew he would find them on the soft stuff we crossed about ten miles in from the boundary."

"In the dark of night?" Jenny was incredulous.

Geoff sighed. "He had his torch, love, with its shaft of light well trained on the ground. Anyway, he went back as far as the boundary grid and found three sets of car-tyre tracks—none of them identical. They were Nat's, Nicole's, and diamond-patterned tracks of the feller who came in and set your Joey loose. That's what all the talk was about, back over by the mulga clump."

Jenny's eyebrows went up.

"You mean to say someone else came this way? But it might only have been someone going up to the homestead."

"Then they were on the wrong track, weren't they?"

"I thought of that myself, when we came in. There were actually three dirt roads leading off from that grid. I wondered then how a stranger would ever know which track to take."

Geoff grinned. "Very observant, aren't you?" he said. "The homestead track is the west one. We took the east track to keep out of Barrett's hair. And our midnight visitor took the east one, too. Now why would he do that? This track leads only here. Then it goes on to the Gibson Desert."

"Perhaps he *was* going out to the Gibson Desert. People do, you know. Geologists and explorers."

"Geologists and explorers don't use an old six-cylinder job; like Drew, they use Land Rovers in rough country."

"How do you know it was an 'old job'?"

"The span of the wheels, the line of oil trailing behind it, and the fact that the back wheels skid an inch or two on right turns."

Geoff went on. "Besides, Drew's been a born tracker all his days," he said. "He can't pass a set of tell-tale tracks without remembering them and checking them out, if he can. It's necessary in his business anyway. If you're collecting pay dirt, you don't tell the world.

So—the upshot of *that* is—he first picked up the track of these diamond-patterned tyre tracks back as far as the Woolagong Roadhouse!"

Jenny had a strange, uneasy feeling. "The man in the white cotton hat!" she said suddenly. "In the shadows by the back path to the kitchen—"

"Whoa!" Geoff said. "Steady on!"

Jenny's spirits were sky-high again. "Drew saw car tracks—radials with a diamond tread? *I* saw a man standing in the shadows. He wore a white cotton hat turned down all round. That's why I noticed him."

Geoff grasped her elbow and turned her about.

"Come and join the party, sweetheart," he said. "Drew's got himself a pearl of a rouseabout and doesn't know it. Ask him for double pay. Let's go and take the blinkers from his eyes."

Still guiding her by her elbow, he led her almost at the run to where Drew and Nicole, squatting down on their heels, were now drawing tracks and plans on the dust.

"Hoi there!" Geoff called. "A female sleuth has come among us. And none of us knew."

Jenny felt better now that her powers of observation were about to prove her useful. Maybe Drew would not leave her out of things any more. She had really been feeling horrid back there by the camp site. Now she was about to be redeemed.

16

Nicole, dusty in her sand-coloured slacks and off-white blouse, looked up in surprise. She stood, shook herself, and then sat down on a log two feet away.

"Really, Geoff," she said, sitting on her throne in judgment. "Jenny does have work to do. We haven't time for games."

"Games?" queried Geoff. He pulled Jenny up hard. Drew, for his part, watched them as if he were mildly irritated by the gambolling of a couple of youngsters.

Geoff swung Jenny round in front of him, held her by both elbows, and propelled her forward so that she was within six inches of Drew, chest to chest.

"Go on, Jenny," Geoff urged from behind. "Tell the boss what you just told me. Go on! Tell him what you saw in the early morning at the roadhouse."

"Yes. Go on, Jenny," Drew spoke quietly, his eyes probing. "What *did* you see at the roadhouse?"

"A man standing in the bushes by the back path to the kitchen—"

"Good heavens!" Nicole drawled, taking out another cigarette and lighting it for herself. "What's so odd about a man? If I remember correctly, there were half a dozen men in the roadhouse that night."

Jenny shook her elbows free of Geoff's grasp. She half turned to Nicole.

"Yes, but they weren't this man, were they?"

"Go on, Jenny," Drew said. "What about this particular man?"

"He was standing back in the bush shadows, as if he

didn't want to be seen. He looked as if he were waiting for something, or someone. Just waiting—"

"Yes. Go on. Why did you take particular note of him?"

"Because of his hat. It was white and very clean. Or maybe just new. I don't know. I hadn't seen anyone in a white hat since we had come up the old Goldfields Road. I noticed that all the men we passed in cars or trucks or Land Rovers wore khaki or jungle-green hats, like the soldiers wear. If there *were* any white ones— well, the dust on that road and along the tracks would soon have covered them with this sort of red-brown dust so that you'd never know they'd ever been white."

"What else did you notice, Jenny?" Drew asked, looking directly at her. "What was this man doing, other than just standing?"

"Nothing. That was what was odd about him, too. He wasn't near a door, or a track-out. He was just standing with that very white hat on his head, the brim pulled down all round."

"To hide his face?"

Probably. That and the bush shadows *did* hide it. But his eyes were very bright. They shone. I know that sounds silly, but—"

Drew was listening attentively. He looked straight into Jenny's face.

"You couldn't identify him, except that his eyes shone and he wore a white hat which no one else around was wearing?"

Was Drew laughing at her? She didn't know, but something about the searching way he was looking at her kindled her spirits again.

"He was odd, and he was out of place," she said carefully. "He held something bright in his hand, I think. But I couldn't see what. It had to be something bright, because the light reflected from it must have been shining in his eyes. Otherwise I wouldn't have been able to see his eyes in those shadows, would I?" She said this last all in one breath. Then she loosened herself from Geoff's grip and moved over to a log near the one Nicole was monopolizing. She sat down with a plonk, as if suddenly released from anxiety as well as custody.

Geoff and Drew exchanged glances.

"He held something bright in his hand?" Drew said thoughtfully. "Not a watch?"

"No," Jenny answered from her log. "His hand— that is, the palm of his hand—was upward."

"How could you possibly see that?" Nicole asked sceptically. "It was only just dawn, and he was in the bush shadows. You *said* you couldn't really see his face, only his eyes."

"Yes," Jenny said. "That is just how it was. Only—"

"Well? *Only*?" Nicole asked again, still sceptical.

"When it is just dawn," Jenny said slowly, "there is a moment of real darkness before the sun begins to rise. Only it isn't the sun that comes first. There is always one ray at least that fairly shoots above the horizon before the others. *Then* comes the rim of the sun."

"We are having a geography lesson." Nicole was amused now.

"Jenny is right," said Geoff. "It doesn't *always* happen, but it *nearly* always happens. First that darkness, then the one ray."

"It happened that morning," Jenny said defensively. "A ray of real yellow light shot across the gap between the kitchen and the outhouse right on the spot where he was standing. It was like a gold pointer. It shone—oh, just for a tiny moment—on his hand. His hand was palm upwards and he had something in it. It was then that his eyes shone. Only for a second or two. After that, the sky was light and the sun began to rise over the eastern sky."

"But you couldn't see what it was that he held in his hand?" Drew asked again. He was very patient now, but extremely interested.

"No. Only that there was a light, and it was shining in his eyes, too."

"Good girl, Jenny," Drew said. "That is a frequent

phenomenon at that hour of the morning. And you noticed it, and also how it happened."

Jenny was struck silent by this unexpected praise. Drew had already turned to Geoff.

"You guess first," he said. "It wasn't his watch because his hand was face upwards, and I've yet to meet anyone who wears his watch on the inside of the wrist in the Outback dust."

"It had to be something small," Geoff said warily. "It could have been the lid of a jam tin—but that is most unlikely. Or maybe it was glass. The only thing I know of that a man on the fringes of the Outback would keep with the glass side upwards is a compass. And that kind of man is a geologist, a miner, or—"

"But," drew said, "what about his hat being white?" If he'd come up the coast with it, it would have already collected dust, red-brown dust at that! Now the stores in Kalgoorlie and Coolgardie do have white cotton hats for sports-minded people. So, getting on with the guesswork, he'd undoubtedly lost his first, probably brown, hat. Nothing unusual about that. However, if he went into the specialty shops in Kalgoorlie or Coolgardie that deal in gear for miners and geologists—if he went into one of *those* to get a new ranger hat, he thought he would be recognized. You with me, Geoff? This part is important."

"Got it!" Geoff agreed. "He didn't want to be recognized or known. Q.E.D., he's been this way before."

"He doesn't want sun-stroke, either, though," Drew added. "So he picks up a tennis or cricketer's sports cap at one of the main town stores, one where he won't be known."

"Rrrright," said Geoff, rolling his r's. "But he carries a compass and is holding it ready for the moment his quarry leaves town, so that he can judge the direction while keeping well behind in order that his dust cloud does not arouse suspicion."

"He knows we are near town," Drew went on musingly. "Watches to see what it's about. Picks up the rumour of the rich 'find' east of the town. Knows of the presence of the safari party. Sees Nat Barrett. Probably takes up a watch by the window and sees us signing with Nat. He doesn't have to be clever to know that Nat Barrett doesn't have opal. So he, this fellow, decides to follow us. We just might be on to something worthwhile, in which case we will peg a claim. Later, he will change our pegs for his own pegs, and beat us back to the Warden's Office to register the claim."

The two men looked at one another. Both were wearing the kind of half-smile that said they now knew everything. Drew particularly, at the moment, wore the air of a lord of the ancient land. He looked around possessively.

Jenny, forgetting Nicole on the other log, had followed the exercise in gold-field logic with great interest. She wished she'd thought it all out herself. But then things weren't quite what they seemed to be on this safari, were they? Gemstones, and opal in particular, were what they were *supposed* to be seeking. Yet, except for Pete the Prospector, she didn't think Drew had attempted to make any other contacts in the region, unless he had done it in the middle of the night. Then what *were* they after? Something the man in the white hat knew about? Had he been waiting in the shadows that early morning, compass in hand, to see in which direction Drew's party would go?

In the midst of these niggling thoughts, she realized—or at least supposed—her own observing eye had been useful. She might even be promoted to the "Council of Equals" and so come to know what they were all up to. These hopes died as quickly as they had been born. She had to be fair. She had applied for the cook-rousabout job and that was the job she had. Whoever presumed to think the kitchen maid should dine with the master? She wasn't one of them *yet*.

But they had arranged for her to share accommodations with Nicole! Besides, they didn't have kitchen maids in this country any more. And although she *was* a runaway girl, she was also a well-educated daughter of a well-known farmer in the deep south!

All the time that the conversation between Drew and Geoff had been continuing, Nicole had been sitting on her log, leisurely smoking her cigarette and watching the others with half-interest. Now she spoke up.

"We'd better give this suspect man a code name, since he doesn't seem to have a known one," she said unexpectedly. "I suggest we call him Whitey. After his hat, of course. Although by this time, that distinguishing part of his apparel ought to be red-brown from dust."

Jenny sat straight-backed on the log. "Excuse me, please," she said. "But could I know if this man's radial-tyre marks have turned up anywhere other than at the roadhouse. I know Drew noticed them there—and at the grid into Mr. Barrett's place."

"His car tracks stopped dead a mile inside Barrett's boundary," Drew said. "I checked last night. But he could have seen our campfire by its glow in the sky and soft-footed it this way. He is what is called in mining circles a *follower*. Some followers sell their information. Others peg claims for themselves."

"If he's the person who tipped Joey out—well, why? Why *Joey*?"

"It must have been the one error all off-beats are likely to make," Geoff said lugubriously. "After all, he had as much right to a camp-down in the bush as we had. But he didn't want a camp-down. He was squizzing. Having done that, and located us for the night—ready to follow on in the morning—he indulges in committing a minor nuisance. He tips up a bag, doubtless thinking it contains nothing of real interest—worn clothes, or somebody's knitting. You jump off your stretcher, he makes off fast—and in a direction other than that which Joey took."

Nicole stood up and brushed her hand down one leg of her slacks.

"Drew, we'd better get on with the day's work, hadn't we?" She sounded as if she were bored to weariness with the troubles of Jenny and Joey. "Now that we know who to watch for."

Drew nodded. Nothing more was said of the strange watcher of the night and Jenny was left to wonder—mostly about the strange ways of people on safari. Each of them—including herself—had something on his or her mind. Yet each one had nothing more to say about it at this moment. Peculiar!

All the same, she had a faint suspicion that Drew, and possibly Nicole, knew who the night visitor might have been—or knew *of* him. And since she herself had played quite an important part in describing this "follower," she felt she, too, was entitled to know who he was.

Oh, well! In a characteristic gesture she threw her hair back over her shoulder as she stood up. Not to know is not to worry, isn't it? So she went back to the clearing up of all that was on and about the camp site.

Geoff, without a goodbye or even a wave of his hand, disappeared along a narrow track that ran through the bush in a northeasterly direction. Drew and Nicole took the Land Rover. It plunged and ricocheted along through the trees in a northwesterly direction. They were clearly off on business of their own.

Jenny supposed—because she had to suppose something—that they were possibly making their own short-cut to Nat Barrett's homestead. Or maybe they were going to meet some contact like Pete the Prospector, who would trade gemstones for hard money.

She had to settle, after all, for not being told anything. But there was quite a lot to do around the camp. And perhaps they'd only be gone for a short while. She had to make up her mind for good that, when it came to the "business" side of the safari, she was not going to be in on it. Why hadn't she woken up to that, once and for all? Maybe it was because she was a farmer's daughter from the deep south and hadn't ever been left out of anything before. That is, anything but the selling of her beloved horse, Redcoat. And she'd run away after *that*.

Jenny fed Joey again, unnecessarily. She had to love

something, and *be* loved by something. Joey was now that something. She felt comforted at the thought.

Back at the camp site she strung a line up between two trees. She washed her own soiled clothes and searched around in Geoff's tent to find those he, too, had discarded. Then she washed these and hung them alongside her own. The line was full now, and two of the big cans of water were empty. Last night Geoff had gone to a waterhole somewhere south of the track on which they had come to the camp site. She would take the cans and replenish them. She was quite confident of her bush sense, and didn't fear the possibility of losing her way.

A water hole was always, in these regions, somewhere among rocks. Jenny took her bearings by the time of day and the bush shadows on the ground, and set off to the south.

The rock pile was less than three hundred yards on the far side of a slow dip in the land. Jenny looked back over her shoulder to mark, by this bent tree and that black stump, the way she had come. By these landmarks she would find her way back. In her mind, she saluted the departed Paul Collett and Geoff for seeing that it had been a bush-trained girl who had finally won the job with the safari. She hoped Drew would ultimately appreciate their choice. She would show them all just how useful she really was, even if she wasn't old enough or wise enough to be taken into their confidence about the safari's ultimate destination.

Jenny had only just turned towards the rock pile again when she saw him—the medium-tall man with the white cotton hat.

It wasn't all that white now, his hat. It had blotches of dust in the side folds. He wasn't wearing it with the brim turned down all the way around now, either. It was still turned down at the front, but the sides were cocked up, and it was those cocked-up sides that were dirt-stained, probably by dusty, heat-greased hands. It was the man, all right.

She was not frightened. She didn't know why she felt

no fear. Probably because she didn't quite believe she was actually seeing him. Talk about him an hour ago, and have him turn up right here? But he *was,* according to Drew, following them! A dozen notions now flashed through her mind, one after the other. Drew and Nicole had recognized her description of this man as she had seen him that early morning outside the roadhouse. She was sure of that. They knew something about him.

As far back as the roadhouse, Drew had been taking note of the radial tread-marks of a vehicle recognized from some time in the past. Drew had *known* they were being followed along their route to Nat Barrett's station. He also had known that some person had tipped up Joey's pouch last night. That was why he had gone seeking tracks in the bush! How strange it all seemed! But Jenny the farm girl wasn't so very surprised. The bushland held no secrets for the experienced bushman!

The man saw that Jenny had seen him. They had both now stopped dead in their tracks, thirty yards apart. They stood looking across a waste of low bush at one another.

Funny, but while she stared at him, Jenny was also noticing and mentally recording everything else that was around them—the red-clay dirt between the bushes, the tired trees on either side, the pile of rocks ahead, looking like unwanted rubble from heaven which some chariot god had emptied out upon the red flat land.

She saw it all, and noted it all; yet her mind was on the man.

"Hey," she said, loud enough for him to hear.

He did not answer. He looked past her as if seeking others who might be behind her. Jenny wanted to ask him why he had tipped Joey's pouch upside down. But common sense prevailed. He probably hadn't even known that the pouch hanging at the opening of her tent had contained a baby kangaroo. So who was he exactly, this follower? And what was he doing now?

Well, the bushland belonged to everybody, didn't it?

Maybe he was just a loner. There were some people in the bush who were like that. Hermits.

But, no! Somewhere he had a car, and it had diamond patterns on its radial tyres. From many, many miles back he had been watching them. No bush-whacker hermit, this one.

And still she was not afraid.

She knew some nasty things, even tragic things, had happened to women on the gold fields in the days when the white man's law was to 'lock up your wives and your daughters; there's a gold rush on!' This was because the glint of gold had brought so many men and mostly *single* men, in search of the Promised Land.

Why was this one following Drew's safari from as far back as Coolgardie? This stranger in the now-dirty white hat could certainly go to the opal fields himself. Everyone knew where they were. It had all been in the papers.

All these thoughts flashed through Jenny's head. And *still* she was not afraid, although she had no idea why not.

"I have two cans of water to fill," she called loudly enough for the man to hear. "You could carry one back to the camp for me."

He did not answer. He simply turned on his heel and walked away into the bush.

Even after she could no longer see him, she could hear his boots crackling through the dried-out undergrowth.

Jenny looked at the shadows on the ground, then at her wrist watch.

He is going southwest, she thought. In a straight line, too.

She bound the sapling stems of a low bush together with her handkerchief, then drew an arrow pointing southwest on the ground below it. She dug tiny bush-ends into the line of the arrow, in case a wind should come up and level away her drawing on the dusty ground.

She then picked up the cans and went sturdily on to the waterhole on the far side of the rocks.

Later, she walked her way back to the camp, now and again putting the cans down to rub the red weals on her hands before taking them up again. There was no one there when she arrived—neither anyone of her own party, nor anyone from the Barrett homestead.

She put the cans of water down in their proper place. Next she went to the pouch hanging from the centre pole of her own tent and took Joey out. She fed him, then sat down by the dead coals of the morning's fire and cradled the little animal close to her. She rested her chin on his soft, furry head and was peaceful.

"Only you and me, Joey," she said, "and a lone man out in the bush. Why doesn't someone come home? It doesn't really matter very much—for a while. It's as if there's only you and me, and the bush, in all the world."

Joey's way of answering was to snuggle his small head deeper under her chin.

They were very comfortable like that.

17

Jenny grew drowsy. Then Joey did, too. They slept there in the shade almost like a young mother and child. Time passed.

Vaguely, in a kind of dream, Jenny heard the heavy tread of boots among the dried grasses and dead, fallen leaves. It was the coming-home sound of a walk-weary man. She was not quite awake yet; nevertheless her inner listening ear registered all sounds new or foreign that broke the midday bush silence.

The wearer of the boots came nearer. Jenny, still in a world of half-sleep, listened to them with comfort. She was dreaming that the warm, breathing thing in her arms was her child and that the feet of the man coming nearer and nearer were those of her good guardian and protector.

The boots stopped. Jenny shook her head and looked up. The figure standing there looking down was very blurry. Then it was clear.

She wiped the daydreams from her eyes with the back of her hand.

"Oh Geoff," she said. "It's only you."

For quite a few seconds he did not answer. Then he shook his own head, as if chasing away some foreign thought.

"Only me?" he asked. "Who were you expecting, Jenny? The man with the white hat, or that fascinating film-star hero of the wilds—Drew Carey?"

Jenny smiled wryly. Then she laughed. "It was you who called him all that, not me! Come to think of it, though—it *is* a rather good description. He *is* hand-some. And he's clever."

"And he's shrewd, but just as designing as the rest of the upper crust. Maybe more artful."

Jenny was wide awake now, and was trying to still Joey, who was showing signs of aggressive restlessness.

"I thought that *you* thought Drew was the tops, Geoff."

"So I do. That doesn't make him perfect, does it? Anyhow who *were* you dreaming about? You had the most seraphic expression on your face."

"Did I?" Jenny ruffled her hair with her spare hand and reached for the pouch lying on the ground two feet away. The only way to still Joey now was to stuff him into the pouch. This she did, and handed the pouch to Geoff. "Hang him up, will you, please? Ouch! I'm stiff."

Geoff hung the pouched Joey to the tent pole while Jenny scrambled to her feet. "You know," she said, shaking herself like a puppy fresh from a cold-water shower, "it was a lovely dream. But I don't know who or what it was about. I've already forgotten. Geoff, why does one forget dreams?"

He moved over to the dead fire, kicked the coals to-gether, picked up a dead bunch of twigs, and scattered them over the fire site. "Probably because dreams are only a matter of wishful thinking." He pushed some dried leaves under the twigs, struck a match, and lit them. He then made a tiny air tunnel under them to force a flare.

"Funny," Jenny said, pushing her fingers through her hair again. "I know it was a lovely dream, all the same. I was so warm and safe."

"Probably thought you were a joey instead of a hu-man being," Geoff said bluntly. "Since you're the cook, and I'm no Joseph in Egypt, how about putting a billy of water on the fire and making us each a cup of tea?"

"Marvellous," Jenny said. She took the blackened billy to one of the cans of water. "Just what I wanted.

Tea. How blessed is tea! That is when one comes in from the outer—"

"You haven't come in from anywhere, Jenny. Not just now, anyway. You've come out of some soporific dream-world where all the cents were dollars and all the men were golden-haired heroes."

Jenny laughed. "That *would* have been fun," she said. Then her laugh faded. Geoff was bending over the new-born fire to position two stones a few inches from one another. He took the billy from her hand and set it on the stones. But he wasn't smiling. Then he looked up at her.

"Girls aren't supposed to look pretty at this hour of the day," he said. "It's just too flaming hot. You and that fool Joey looked like you had just come out of a cool shower and were about to deal only with the kind of people who inhabit heaven—if there is such a place."

Jenny was delighted. "Oh Geoff, you *are* turning poetical! I always *knew* you had something more in you than just he-man bossiness."

"Thank you. Your approval is welcomed. Now will you please stop talking and fetch the tea leaves? And after that, fetch some of that tinned fruit cake we brought in hundred-weights all the way from Kalgoorlie."

Jenny did as she was told. Back to being put in my place, she thought. But I'd just better remember to make a damper cake in the fire coals after dinner tonight. Even *I* can get tired of tinned fruit cake!

They sat, each on a mat of leaves, and at opposite sides of the fire.

When the tea drinking was finished, Jenny reached for a long stick and stirred the fire. She then separated the coals from one another. Next, with the knob end of the stick, she pushed sand high round each coal; it was a safety precaution in the afternoon of a day which by any standard was very hot.

"Quite a dab at doing that, aren't you?" Geoff said.

"I learned it as a child. So did you. A loose fire in

forest country does you know what. It can even burn a whole town out."

"What else did you—we—learn in the guilt-free days of childhood?"

"Guilt-free?" Jenny asked, startled. "What an odd thing to say! I don't know about *you*, but me? I *always* had a guilty conscience about something. Like coming in late for dinner, or forgetting something important when I did the shopping. Once I rode Redcoat through the Naylors' newly seeded paddock. Redcoat took the fence—plus the jamwood forest! Because I let him, of course. But I didn't know the Naylors had seeded. Golly, was there a ringing of telephones and tough words from both ends before *that* little 'do' was over, let alone forgotten—! Jenny broke off. Her gaze strayed over the low scrub and across the spinifex plain beyond. The sparse bushland behind her was very quiet.

"Such a silence," she said unexpectedly.

Geoff poked the dead fire coals with *his* stick this time. Then he looked up at Jenny. Her mind was far away. Her eyes were not seeing the blue grass or the dried-out claypan over to the west or even the clump of salmon gums bordering the track past the camp.

She's back home at Yaraandoo, Geoff thought—back by the pony paddock with a nifty Arab steed called Redcoat!

He reached across the distance and snapped his fingers in front of her eyes.

"Wake up, chick," he said. "You were the one who wanted to come away. Now you're here; so you'd better like it."

"I'm not homesick, if that is what you are thinking," Jenny answered. "Actually I was wondering—well, some of the time anyway—when Drew and Nicole will be back. Maybe we should keep the coals glowing. Drew will want a pint billy of tea, at least."

Geoff had tucked his chin in. He looked at her from under levelled brows.

"And not Nicole?" he asked.

"Nicole? Of course," Jenny said. "When I think of Drew I automatically think of Nicole, too."

"So all that day-dreaming by camp sites is about Drew plus Nicole?"

Jenny, angry now, threw a nut at him.

"And what if it is?" she asked, head in the air.

"Then stop it. You'll only get hurt, Jenny," he said, gently now. "The world they live in is a foreign one to us. Think about camp recipes, or maybe Joey—if you must. Or about what sort of sunset you'll get each night against that western sky. But leave those two be."

Jenny's back was very straight, and her chin well in the air.

"You've been wanting to say that to me almost since we started out, haven't you? Well, we may come from the same place, Geoff, but you are not my keeper."

"Not yet, anyway," he said, quite meaningfully, but with his face easing into a grin. "I kind of thought when we started out I might have to keep a leg-rope and halter on the girl from Yaraandoo. And now, since last night's adventure down an old mine shaft and to-day's adventure with the man in the white hat, not to mention your falling asleep with a pet kangaroo in your arms next to a fire which was still hot at sand level—"

"The man in the white hat?" Jenny asked, startled, "How did *you* know I saw him today? I meant to tell you, only then you started teasing me. As for falling asleep—Oh, blow you, Geoff! You make me feel stupid. I'm not frightened of that man. He's a nut. I'm sure of that. Just a nut. Why don't we stop thinking about him?"

Geoff made no reply. So Jenny repeated her first question. "How *did* you know I saw that man today?"

"I was coming through the bush from the other side. I saw him going off and you looking after him. Then you took the cans to the rock hole."

"Why, for goodness sake, didn't you call out? Or come and help me with those huge cans? Filled with water they are very, very heavy, you know."

"Yes, I do know. I also remember how strong those

hands of yours are. So I thought it was better to follow Whitey and see just what *he* was up to. Very important that."

"Well, must I wait till Drew and Nicole come home to hear what you *did* find out about him? He doesn't frighten *me*, you know. There's something a bit sad and all alone about him "

"You keep away from that sad-and-all-alone type out here in the gold fields, Jenny," Geoff said severely. "They can be the worst. All the same, I'm with you; I don't think this chap is dangerous, either. He's working bigger stakes—and for someone else, I'm inclined to think. So he wouldn't be likely to be taking time off for play."

Jenny ignored the implications of this last remark.

"How far did you follow him?" she asked.

"As far as his car, and that wasn't so far at all. He had it stashed behind another rock pile about a half-mile from the water hole. And guess what?"

"No, you tell me. I never was good at guessing games."

"His car tracks were made by radial tyres, all of them with a diamond pattern."

"Oh Geoff, aren't you clever!" Jenny said, laughing now. Then she stopped. "But where does that leave us?"

"We let Drew figure that one out," Geoff said shortly. "The important point is that he is definitely following *us*. On the track and off it, he's right behind us. But he also makes silly mistakes, like tipping up somebody's pouch bag as it hangs from the top rope of a tent pole. I'd guess he's the sort of chap who'd pick a neighbour's sprig of wattle from over the fence as he passed by and not care a fig whether he's seen or not. And I'll make another guess about him—that he bought those flash tyres to compensate for not being able to buy a flash car. You know what he's driving? An outdated, hard-top saloon six-cylinder job that badly needs a quart of paint. Correct that. It's a two-tone outdated Holden; so what it needs is two *two*-pint tins, one of pale green and one of pale yellow. You see, Jenny, a two-tone vehicle of any make is more noticeable than a one-colour job because—"

Jenny stamped her foot. "Geoff, don't keep on teasing. That *is* what you are doing, isn't it? Explaining unnecessary details to the child?"

"Unnecessary details, my foot! Jenny, do you know what that six-cylinder hard-top *was* before it went to the used-car dealer, and before that same used-car dealer painted it in two tones to hide its history? What's most different about it from other cars on the road? Come on, Jenny. Tell me."

"I hope you don't mean it was once a hearse," Jenny said uneasily.

"No. But you're getting near. Give it another try."

Jenny wrinkled her brow, looked through the trees, then brought her eyes back to Geoff's face. He was looking kindly at the moment. Something warmed in her heart. Dear old Geoff! she thought. She nearly forgot what it was she had in mind to say. Then she recalled it.

"Oh yes, I know," she said happily. "A police van! The kind that has blue lights that flash, and stops the speeders—"

"Quite right. Go to the top of the class. Now, question two. Do the police sell their outdated, getting-old jobs to used-car dealers? Because that is where this one came from. Whitey couldn't have afforded anything else. He has holes in the soles of his boots, you know. They show up in his footprints. And nobody, but *nobody*, walks in the prickly Australian bush or over a spinifex strip with holes in his boots—not if he wants his feet to carry him anywhere safe to tell the tale!"

Drew and Nicole came back to the camp an hour later. With them came Nat Barrett. Jenny immediately started up the fire again. Nat Barrett, she discovered, had a very nice smile, which she had not much noticed at the roadhouse.

Heavens! she thought as she smiled back in answer

to his greeting. Was it so short a time ago? It seemed as if ages had passed since then.

She offered to make tea. Drew half-smiled his assent and raised his eyebrows in Nat Barrett's direction. It was his shorthand way of asking if Nat, too, would like tea. Nat nodded, and Nicole said, "Of course!" Then the three of them had immediately fallen into some low-toned conversation with Geoff.

The "Council of Three" has become the "Council of Four," Jenny thought. She felt quite pleased with herself for being able to label them so aptly. It made her feel less isolated. Oh! If only she were twenty instead of eighteen! Why hadn't she put up her age? Perhaps she could try a different hair style. That, at least, would make her *look* older—perhaps old enough to be included in the party on equal terms.

Tea was made and being consumed together with more tinned fruit cake, all to the tune of small talk.

Jenny was actually beginning to enjoy herself when a nasty thought assailed her. Were they waiting for her to go away so they could go on talking about what they had probably been discussing all afternoon? She jumped up, shook cake crumbs around for the birds, and said, "Excuse me, please. I have to look over the stores."

From behind the canvas-covered stores she peered out to see what really did go on. Well, the "Council of Four" was not talking about important things at all. Nat Barrett was obviously entertaining the others with bushwacker tales, the other three were smiling, and every now and again Geoff would give a positive hoot of laughter. Once or twice he even slapped his side.

Why didn't I stay? Jenny thought. Perhaps they didn't want me to go at all!

Well, the stores did have to be checked and tidied up every two or three days anyway. So why not today and be done with it? Also, within the next half hour, Joey would have to be fed. "Thank God for little Joey," she said to herself. This last thought warmed her heart. Indeed, Joey already seemed to know her. When she lifted him out of the pouch and held him under one arm while she turned the pouch inside out to air, Joey nuzzled into her side and stayed put, no longer struggling to get away.

Every now and again, as the others continued to chat, Jenny would look up from whatever she was doing and gaze across at them.

At one point Nat Barrett took out some charts from the deep flap-pocket of his safari jacket, spread first one and then another on a flat stone, and began indicating something. Jenny could actually see his forefinger travelling across a page. Then he and Nicole apparently exchanged views while Drew and Geoff listened.

Maybe we're going some place new, Jenny thought hopefully.

She was right. The next day they broke camp and set off in a northeasterly direction. Timber was sparser, and the gibber stones more plentiful—all over the place, in fact.

Twice, as they travelled, they met a prospector waiting at the track side for their party. Each time the same procedure took place: stones were exhibited and Drew took out his wallet.

Nicole in her now very dusty car was the leader. Drew followed in second place, and then came Jenny with Geoff in the Land Rover.

"Nicole to lead the way because she knows it," Geoff said. "Drew to follow and control the heaviest of the loads over these dratted dirt tracks. Me last to apply the spanner when either vehicle in front overheats its engine or blows a tyre."

"Nicely organized," Jenny said, assuming a tone of admiration. "No mention of my name, of course. I guess I'm just a hanger-on."

The Rover swerved to avoid a pot hole, and the outside wheels jolted on the broken edge of the track. Jenny grasped the door strap to keep herself steady.

Geoff glanced at her and grinned. "You said it," he said. "Note how you suit actions to words."

Jenny let go of the door strap as if it had been an adder.

"One day," she said balefully, "when all this is over and we get back to Yaraandoo, I'll pay you back for your lack of chivalry—and with interest!"

"Come the day!" Geoff said cheerfully. Then the expression on his face changed. "I'll have made enough to set up my own block of land by then. When we get to where we are going right now, Jenny, take that dilly-bag of yours and bag a few gemstones for yourself. That'll pay the cost of fencing the block. I'll pay you back with a good Arab steed."

"An Arab steed! As if anything Arab, or even Palomino, could replace Redcoat! So, I am to fence your block for you?" Jenny asked.

"You don't like the idea?" Geoff glanced down at her.

"Well—" Jenny said thoughtfully. "That *would* make me useful, wouldn't it? You would take me into your confidence about what kind of fence you'd like and how much it would cost of course."

"Certainly."

"Then you would be telling me more then than you are telling me now. For instance, exactly *where* are we heading right this minute?"

"Dunno," Geoff said, very lugubrious. "Drew's orders were to follow his dust and stop when he stops. I said I would. Right now I'm doing exactly that."

Jenny fell silent. She was thinking about Drew now. She still had that exciting feeling of being drawn to him. Yet somewhere deep inside her a seed of doubt had begun to grow. Every now and again she found herself longing for him to show again that quiet attractiveness that had been magic for her at the beginning of the safari. Now he was too preoccupied. But with what? It had to be Nicole, she supposed.

They had been travelling about two hours when they

came to the Wayside House—a lone store for long-distance travellers following the by-tracks to the main highway. The only evidence of plant life, other than the spinifex and some mulga, was a circular plantation of trees around an enormous windmill and tank. But on either side of the wattle-and-daub store building was sparse lawn and riots of bougainvillea.

"Underground water!" Geoff said. "The great wonder of the Australian Outback. Sometimes there's enough water to grow a banana plantation.

Jenny only said, "Mm," because her mind was on other things—namely Drew's vehicle, parked under a very old pepper tree. But there was no Nicole or Mercedes Benz. Even as they pulled up, she could see only the top of Drew's head; he was beyond a petrol bowser, filling his Cruiser with petrol.

"Hiya!" Geoff said as he passed Drew and a white-haired man who was pouring oil in the car.

"Don't take long," Drew said as Geoff passed him.

"Shan't," said Geoff equally laconic. "I'll fill up next stop-over. Just want to get some coffee from the store."

Jenny eased herself out of the Rover. She wanted to stretch her legs. She smiled hopefully at Drew but he was too busy shutting down the bonnet of his car to notice it.

"Tell Geoff to skip the first fork in the road and take the second," he said.

"Yes, of course." Jenny couldn't think of anything else to say. As she went through the entrance of the store she caught a glimpse of a shabby, dusty Overlander parked down by the far side of the building.

She went into the store and towards the counter. A youngish woman came in from the back areas with two bottles of orange drink and a package of sandwiches. This order was for Geoff. At that moment Jenny glanced at four men, youngish except for one, who were all sitting at a side table just around the corner of the counter. A meagre plate of sandwiches on the table was apparently being shared between them. One of the men picked up the next to last sandwich, broke it in

half, and passed one half to another, shorter man. Even
without thinking about it, Jenny registered the fact that
it was a very small lunch for four males. She also noticed that one man drew on a cigarette belonging to another. None of them wore hats. If they had them they
had stuffed them into their belts or left them in that old
jalopy down by the side of the store. Jenny noticed all
these things, particularly the sharp way they had taken
in Geoff and everything about him. They had all followed him with their eyes as he went out of the door.

There was something familiar about one of them,
Jenny thought—the one whose shoulders were lower
than those of the other three as they sat there at that
small table.

Jenny did not know why she was a noticing person.
But the habit of it had certainly been useful, she
thought, especially that time when she had noticed that
Whitey (as he was now named) had held his palm up
and had had a shine in his eyes. It had been those two
observations of hers which had led Drew to the conclu-
sion that Whitey had been holding a compass—

Jenny's thoughts jumped several sentences. A *compass!*

Had he needed the compass to find his way because
he didn't know it? She had seen him first at the roadhouse and then at the bush camp; they had been travelling north then. But they were travelling northeast
now—a direction which led only to the Gibson Desert.

There would be no more stopovers, no petrol stations, no stores for provisions. There was nothing ahead
but blue grass, spinifex, and an occasional clump of
mulga or salmon gum.

Her thoughts came back to base.

So this place right here was the last stopover, the
very last, unless one turned due north. There *was* a
road that way; it was on the map.

And the man she saw over there—the one whose
shoulders were lower than those of the others and who
had nothing to eat in front of him—just *could* be
Whitey. No hat—white, brindle *or* brown—was in evi-

dence; so she had to do some guessing. But this man had a sort of round face, eyes that looked out from under the brows as if forever watching, and somewhat sloping shoulders—all of which checked out.

Then why didn't he flicker his eyelids just a little bit when she looked at him directly, eye to eye? The other three were staring at her too, and their eyes did not flicker, either. But somehow—for no good reason at all, except instinct—she was sure he *was* Whitey.

So she smiled at him, a small smile only.

He did not return it.

So she turned away to the counter, where the young woman was holding a packet of sandwiches and indicating the cartons of cold coffee.

Jenny took the five steps required to reach the counter, whereupon the tallest man at the table stood up, pushed his chair back quietly, and came to the counter quickly. He stood very close to her and, when she opened her purse to pay, he leaned over her shoulder and peered into it. She partly turned to look at him, holding her purse tight because she thought he meant to snatch it.

"Quite a lot of money you have there," he said lightly, as if that fact, and that fact alone, was what mattered.

"Only small change," Jenny said. She was fibbing, because the folded dollar notes were in a zipped-up side pocket of the purse.

The man put his hand on Jenny's shoulder quite firmly, although not unkindly. It occurred to her he was detaining her rather than meaning to rob her.

18

The glass door opened and someone almost catapulted in. She had never seen anything so fast in her life. It was Geoff, but not a Geoff Jenny had ever known. He seemed taller, his shoulders were braced back, his arms crossed in front of his chest.

"Get out! Into the Rover!" he snapped at Jenny, not taking his eyes from the big man for an instant. Every inch of her knew that something was wrong, really wrong. She felt it in her skin and the roots of her hair.

The three men still at the table had pushed back their chairs and were standing belligerently. Yet they did not move.

It would be four to one against.

"*Out!*" Geoff commanded Jenny.

She did as she was told. She walked quietly to the glass door, pushed it open, and went out into the midday sun. She hefted herself into the driver's seat of the Rover. Only then did she turn and look through the great plate-glass window of the store. Geoff was standing as before, his feet slightly apart and his arms folded high across his chest. Jenny from down-south forest knew what that stance meant. Those folded arms could swing up in an instant to protect face and head from a hard blow.

Suddenly, with whip-lash speed, Geoff lifted one foot and tumbled the chair immediately in front of him. Then with a sort of sliding speed he was at the door, through the door, and into the Rover's open door on the driver's side. At the same time, Jenny slipped into the passenger seat, a bit awkwardly because of the gear casing.

She had had the engine running. All Geoff had to do was let go of the brakes and move into travelling gear.

They were racing down the road in no time.

"I don't believe it!" said Jenny, after a short, cold silence. "I just don't believe it—happened."

"It happened all right." Geoff was very grim. Jenny could tell that by the set of his mouth.

"But why? I didn't have much money."

"They weren't after your money. That was a feint. They were after a disturbance. They might have attacked you, who knows?"

"But *why?*"

"So that one of them could make a getaway behind the blind of a tussle with you. As a matter of fact, one of them did.

Jenny was still puzzled. This sort of adventure, if she could call it that, happened to other people, not to Jenny Haseltine. It belonged on TV or in films.

"I don't believe it," she said again, still bewildered. "It was all so quick. Did it really happen?"

"If you say that once more, I'll open the passenger door and bundle you out." Geoff spoke almost as if he meant it.

"Why be cross with *me?* I didn't do anything—anything *wrong*, I mean."

"You did something which is profoundly silly, in gold country, let alone precious-gem country. You went into a place where there were only strange men. Don't ever do that again. Next time you might get hurt."

They were silent for some time. Jenny was thinking how fearless Geoff had been against those four men. Four against one. Then, out of nowhere, she remembered something else.

One of the men—the short one—had gone. Through the window? Out the back way? She didn't know. When Geoff had hustled her to the door, there had been the four strange men in the room. When she had glanced back, there had been only *two* men at the table and one other standing.

"It was Whitey who disappeared," she said suddenly. "I never saw him close up or without a hat. The one sitting down at the window side! I *know*. At least I *think*—"

"Good. Go up to the top of the class."

"From where?" Jenny demanded with some indignation.

"The bottom, of course."

"Geoff, I don't think that's fair play. For years and years and years we've argued and sometimes quarrelled —that is when we were very young. But we've always played fair."

Geoff's manner softened. "Quite right," he said. "Apologies." He still did not look at her. His gaze was unwavering—straight in front of him.

Jenny said, "Thank you," in a very low voice. She would have liked to touch him, just lightly, to show her real feelings, but this she could not do.

"You know something?" Geoff said, after a long silence.

"No. You tell me."

"Looking after you is some problem. You don't have any experience of the Outback, which is quite different from farming country in the fertile south. It's small town, down there; you know everyone and everyone knows you—so you're relatively safe, no matter where you go or what you do. But that's not the case around here. On top of that, you have a mind of your own. How does a feller take care of a girl like that?"

Jenny thought of a quick retort, but let it pass. She wasn't sure that Geoff mightn't be right. She'd never thought of herself in that way before. Maybe all her troubles in the past *had* stemmed from having a mind of her own. Maybe she *shouldn't* have ridden Redcoat at a gallop through the thick of the bush and worried everybody; there *might* have been a rabbit hole, or a piece of loose fencing wire, that even Redcoat would not see. As for John, he was ambitious and very strict, to the point of sometimes appearing to be a hard man. Maybe her parents genuinely had thought he would be good for their harum-scarum Jenny! She thought they were wrong and had run away to prove it. But now, right here in the far Outback—! The gold-framed watch she wore! And the purse bespangled with golden trim that she was carrying! What would she had done without Geoff? But he was utterly fearless! Oh, Geoff. Dear Geoff.

Suddenly, Jenny was feeling very, very humble.

"Geoff," she said. "Nicole has sometimes gone off in that car on her own. I've always been either with you or Drew. Did Drew tell you part of your job was to watch over me and keep me out of trouble?"

Geoff's grin was a very small one. "He did."

"Right from the start?"

"Right from the start."

"That is why you were always back at the camp before them—and all that?"

"And all that!" Geoff agreed. "That and one other reason, which I'll tell you another day."

There was then a very long silence while Jenny battled to keep back angry tears. She had not wanted to be a weight on anyone's mind, least of all Geoff's.

They had come such a long way, and Geoff had always had to stay behind to keep on looking after her. What a nuisance he must find her!

And actually, he'd been so nice about it—pretending to be companionable and everything! Each day, Drew and Nicole had shot off somewhere, probably to meet the prospectors who sold Drew their gems, or to join in some venture with Nat Barrett. And Geoff had known all about those madly interesting activities but had had to stick around. Underneath his air of comradeship he had probably been whipping his own brand of cat because he had pressed for her to get the job. Part of the reason Caroline had been the first choice must have been that originally she and her parents had come from the Outback! She knew the way of it. Jenny, on the other hand, was a small-town girl who fell down mineshafts and hob-nobbed with "baddies" at stop-overs!

Jenny felt so sad. She would have liked to put her head on Geoff's shoulder and have him say something reassuring to her. She wondered what it would be like to do just that.

But he just drove on not once looking at her or saying a word of any kind.

So, all right! She'd made her own bed and must now lie in it. She would be the best camp cook ever! She would do every single little two-cent job around the place to perfection!

She leaned her head against the windowpane and began to dream up recipes and new ways of making the camp comfortable. She would keep all the tents clean and tidy (even Nicole's)—but especially Geoff's.

Geoff swerved the Rover around a wide bend, and they passed a petrol station. Civilization again! Next came small houses and wide-fenced, dry-grassed paddocks. A single-track railway line now ran parallel to the road.

They then found themselves driving along the main street of a small Outback town. There were dusty or muddy Land Rovers everywhere—but especially outside the single-story hotel. Here and there Jenny saw dusty men in khaki hats, khaki shorts, khaki shirts, and yellow miners' boots—talking to one another or weaving their way towards the hotel.

Best of all, there was a threesome talking together in front of an office-like building with Warden's Court written outside it on a large wooden notice. It was Drew, Nicole, and Nat Barrett! They were all smiling and joking with one another, very pleased with themselves.

Geoff continued to head down the main street, looking for a place to park the Rover. As he slowed down, he glanced in the rear-vision mirror. His grin was suddenly so wide that Jenny was startled. She leaned sideways to see into the mirror herself. What was it that had made Geoff suddenly look so pleased with himself?

Coming round the wide bend into the main street was that two-toned jalopy which, at one time in its history, might have been a police car.

Geoff slowed down almost to a stop and waited. He continued to watch in the rear-vision mirror as the old jalopy slowed down. Its driver was looking for a space outside that Warden's Court in which he could park his vehicle. Jenny could now see his crew, the four men last seen at the stopover.

Geoff angled the Rover in among other Rovers, opened the door, and hoisted himself out. He took cigarettes and matches from his pocket and then leaned over the car bonnet, resting his elbows on it as he lit his cigarette.

He didn't say one word but, as he rested on that bonnet and drew on the cigarette, he wore the expression of one who has joyfully bested his prey.

Jenny opened the passenger door, eased herself out, and stood looking in the direction from which they had come. She could not be seen by the driver and passengers of the old jalopy because she was partly hidden by a line of parked Rovers.

This time the four men from the stopover were wearing their hats. Three of them were *khaki*-colored cotton, as befits men of the Outback. But one man, dusty and earth-stained, wore a cotton hat that must once have been white, although it was so no longer.

"*Whitey!*" Jenny exclaimed, more to herself than to the world at large. "I can't go *anywhere* without seeing that man somewhere around."

Geoff, still leaning on the bonnet of the car behind her and drawing pleasurably on his cigarette, just laughed.

"But it's who gets to the Warden's Court first that matters," he said. Then he stood up, straightened himself, and held out his hand to Jenny. "Come and join the others—Nicole and Drew. They're now in that pub celebrating. They're out of court and have the Miners' Right all tied up in legal ribbon."

Jenny wanted to ask, "What Miners' Right?" But

there were too many people milling about in the pub even to hear herself speak. Clearly today was a day of days in this very important but tiny Outback town. It was the day the Warden's Court sat to hear mining claims and rights taken out or transferred. In the sixties the claims and rights had been mainly for nickel. Now, this year the clamor was all for gold.

Gold on the world market was at its all-time high. A new Gold Boom would begin any day now. Meantime everyone who had the know-how and the chance was securing his lease. In on the ground floor—that, Geoff said, was exactly what the triumvirate of Drew, Nicole, and Nat Barrett had been about from the time they'd left that down-south town in the forest country till this afternoon. The safari had been a camouflage, and the opal prospects a side track, too. It had all been to cover up what Drew Carey was really after. *Gold!*

19

Nat Barrett saw Jenny and Geoff first, and called across the room "Hoi! Come and get it!" *It* was a pint-pot of Goldfields ale. Geoff, guiding Jenny through the press of bodies, was saying "Hallo!" here, and "Hallo!" there. But he did not introduce Jenny to anyone. Instead, he ordered a half-and-half for her, shouting over heads to the barman. He grasped the pot of ale Nat had offered, lifted it first to Nat and then to Drew and Nicole—who were ten bodies away. "Here's luck!" He almost had to shout to be heard across the din. "You beat the other lot by half a day!"

To Jenny, Drew seemed to have changed character altogether. He was leaning against a pillar that supported part of the roof, and he was smiling wide and happy. Jenny didn't think that sort of a grin suited him the way Geoff's grin suited Geoff. But then she had always known Geoff. So his grin was part of her life, just like the rest of him was—even down to his bossiness about keeping her out of dangerous situations.

Somebody passed Jenny's half-and-half over the many heads and safely into her hands. She made a silent wish upon her first sip. Her wish was that when Drew and Nicole went off to enjoy themselves, they would detail Geoff to keep an eye on *her*.

Geoff quietly and steadily shouldered himself through the crowd to Drew's side. Once there, he appeared to be hearing better-than-good news in detail.

Strangely, it was Nicole who edged her way to Jenny's side. Her smile was so bright, eager, and genuine that Jenny felt that Nicole—yes, *Nicole!*—was a different person. She touched Jenny's glass with hers and said, " 'Lucky Lot'—that's what we're going to call the mine, when we get it going. 'Lucky' because Nat's men staked out the strike accurately. And 'Lot' because we played it canny all the way up from the south, gave the 'followers' the slip, and arrived at the Warden's Court before they even knew quite where we'd pegged. There's been one or another of them tracking Drew for weeks. Up here you can't even stake your back-yard without some news leaking out. That's why we made a hoo-haa about a gemstone hunt, because Drew's a known collector in that field." She laughed, and Jenny wondered why she had not seen the liveliness in Nicole before.

"So—this strike? Is it really gold? And is it yours now?"

"Of course it's ours. The Company's, I mean—" Nicole paused to take two sips from her glass. "And it's real gold—not copper pyrites looking like it, but the real thing! A major strike. We hit it six months ago, but we had to wait, of course, till it was mapped and evaluated. Nat, being on the spot, had that particular job. We took over in the southwest to head off suspicion of what we were doing."

Jenny sipped from her glass. "Excuse me," she said, "but would you please tell me why this company started its safari down at Yaraandoo. Why Yaraandoo?"

"We remembered Geoff coming from that place. We've had him on a real gemstone safari before! And we needed a safari type who could look after the vehicles on the mechanical side. So we had the well-known wizard, Paul Collett, set us up from there. Then all we needed was a cook-rouseabout."

Nicole lifted her glass as if to give Yaraandoo a toast in the person of Jenny.

"So I came," Jenny said, rather quietly. "All the time I thought it was for opal—"

"Oh, opal!" Nicole scoffed, removing that precious gem from consideration. "You can pick that up in any side store in Sydney or Melbourne. That is, if you can afford it. But you know, Jenny, we *did* have to have a cover. And what better luck than that the newspapers were full of an opal strike east of Kalgoorlie! Of *course* we gave it out that *that* was what we were after!"

20

Jenny wanted to be glad, but somehow she felt sad. They were all frauds then—Drew and Nicole and Paul Collett! Well, she did have to concede that this was how things were done in the prospecting and mining world. Perhaps it was from necessity. She was glad for Drew and Nicole and Nat Barrett that now they might start a gold mine. She knew enough, though, to know that first it would cost them a lot of money to set up the actual workings. But she supposed they had it. Nicole had the reputation of being rich. And Drew wouldn't have been able to afford the many safari trips he'd been on as a gem collector unless somewhere behind him there was money.

Jenny took another sip from her glass.

"What about Geoff?" she asked, hoping the crack in her voice was not apparent over the noise in the room. "Did he know we were after gold and not opal?"

"Not till we were sure we were being followed. We had to bring him in then. One more pair of eyes. We chose routes that might throw off the follower, but he was faster than we thought. We suspected he was on to us at the roadhouse. And knew for sure when he took a close look-see round our camp and was stupid enough to tip out your Joey. That's when we told Geoff. I suppose that at first the follower hoped we would lead him to the location of our strike. Then, towards the end, he and his pals were just trying to delay us."

Jenny hardly heard the end of what Nicole was saying. She all but spilt her drink as she clapped one hand over her mouth.

"Joey!" she said, her eyes full of concern." Who's going to feed him? I should have——"

She turned her head and found Drew almost at her shoulder.

"Drinking to our good fortune, Jenny?" he asked. Jenny stared at him—half of her still worrying about Joey, and the other half wondering how she had ever fallen for him. Oh yes, he was nice. And when he smiled his eyes were marvellous. But—all those tricky ways of doing things! Well, maybe they had to be done that way. (For the life of her, she could not marshall her thoughts properly). But where had honour gone?

She looked round quickly. "Where's Geoff?" she demanded. "Where did Geoff go?"

"Looking for a port in the storm, Jenny?" Drew asked.

"No. Well, yes. Where *has* Geoff gone, please? I'm sure he'll take me back to feed Joey. That is, if I ask him——" She could not confess to him that Geoff was the one in this strange world she needed most.

"No need to worry about Joey," Drew said casually. "Nat Barrett has a menagerie back of the old homestead on his run. That's where I intended to take Joey in the first place. And Nat says he could use another kangaroo."

"You were taking Joey to—Mr. Barrett's place?" Jenny asked slowly, not believing it. She had thought the joey was to be hers.

Drew smiled. She knew that he knew exactly what was going on in her head and was putting it down—this discovery of hers—to learning about life the hard way. But why couldn't he have told her in the first place that the joey was going to his mining partner?

Nicole had turned away to speak to two people who had come up to greet her. Jenny was left staring rather hopelessly at Drew. He had a "kind uncle" expression on his face as he looked back at her.

"Where would you keep a joey, Jenny?" he asked. "Especially when it had grown? They grow *big*. You'd have to give it to some zoo or menagerie in the fullness of time. And Nat's is as good a one as any. It's in the animal's natural habitat to begin with—"

Jenny pulled herself together. She was accepting the fact that mining entrepreneurs had to be two-faced to be successful. Was it also necessary in the care of a baby kangaroo? All he had really had to do was be honest with her. But it apparently just wasn't in his make-up, in his character.

"Yes," she said at last. "I understand. But Joey *does* need to be fed tonight. He is only a baby. Drew, please! Do you know where Geoff has gone?"

Drew wiped his hand across his chin.

"Like the man who's 'gone fishin' when he's most needed, I suspect he's gone to see a man about a horse. In other words, he's off on business of his own." Drew took Jenny's elbow and turned her round to face the bar—a glory of carved bric-a-brac dating back from the first gold boom almost a hundred years ago.

"This way!" he said, ignoring her concern about Geoff's whereabouts. "Coming, Nicole? Good. We'll have another drink all around and get to the shower rooms before any of the other 'permanents' stake a claim. By the way, Jenny, we're staying here overnight. Nat will send his eldest son over to our camp site to get the joey. And if Geoff stays missing, that's *his* lookout, isn't it?"

Jenny felt sadly rebellious but knew now that that was part of being only eighteen. Oh, well! She was in the world of the big mining people, wasn't she? Even the dustiest face under the dustiest of khaki cotton hats might hide a millionaire—a *gold* millionaire.

All the same she wished she knew where Geoff was. She realized she had become *used* to Geoff being round and about; now she needed him.

"Excuse me, miss." A male voice accosted her. "You'd be with that party came in a while back? I mean in that Land Rover, five down the line?"

He was a tall, brown, leathery man with a stockman's stetson parked on the back of his head.

Jenny looked and counted five Land Rovers down the line. It *could* be Geoff's Land Rover.

"I'm not quite sure—"

"Tall fellow in Nat Barrett's party—light brown hair."

Drew's hair was not light brown. So he must mean Geoff.

Geoff? Yes, that would be his Land Rover. Oh, if only she knew where he'd gone! She wanted no one else. Only Geoff. Oh, Geoff! With him lay safety. And truth.

"You all right, miss?"

"Perfectly."

"You look a bit tired. Touch of the sun maybe. Guess you've come a long way today. More'n a hundred miles, I hear. That Geoff what's-his-name comes spry, though, doesn't he? Well, Nat Barrett told me that when this Geoff chap came into town—I was to take him out to the station. Well, he went in the pub first. But when he came out he was rarin' to go. So I took him out to the station; it's only a few miles out. Then this chap, this Geoff, told me to come right back here and he'd follow after himself. So I thought I'd just better report that he's coming maybe any minute now. Something was really getting him. He was sort of excited, I'm telling you! *Mad* to get goin'."

"But—I don't understand." Jenny was bewildered and lost, as if she were a child again. Why did Geoff want to come back alone? Was someone else bringing him?

As if in answer to her unspoken question, the man added, "It's something to do with a horse, Miss. I guess he's riding that horse back."

"A *horse?*" Jenny was incredulous.

"Yes, that's right." Drew's voice came from behind her. "He's bringing in a horse."

Jenny swung round.

Drew was standing there, cigarette in one hand, the other hand in his pocket. Nicole was not in sight.

"But what's he doing with a *horse*?" Jenny asked, completely puzzled.

Drew put out his cigarette and threw the stub into the trash can at the side of the road. "Well," he said quietly, "We—that is, Nicole, Nat, and myself, plus sundry daughters and one wife, who all belong to Nat—had set up this Exploration Company. Now that the strike has been confirmed, and we've had a successful reaction from the Warden's Court, we thought the two members of the safari who did not hold any shares should have some reimbursement—that is, something beyond the usual wages." His eyes were holding hers. What was bothering Jenny was that now she didn't see anything special in those eyes; they were quite nice, but that was all. She couldn't understand how she'd been so mesmerized by them earlier.

"Therefore—" Drew's voice did sound as if something about to happen to Jenny was going to be a considerable surprise.

Well, she could tell him, if he wanted to know, that nothing would ever be big enough really to surprise her again, not after the surprises she had encountered on *this* safari.

"Are you with me, Jenny?" Drew asked. She nodded. "Nat's neighbour on Sandhill Station had a fine animal. He'd only had it a few months; but now he's selling it again. We heard about your having lost your pet horse, and seeing how attached you were to the joey, and because Nat was taking the joey over for his menagerie—we thought we would give you this horse as your share of the reward for helping us to success." He paused, then went on. "Now say nothing, Jenny—just yet. And take that anxious expression from your face. Geoff was in on it, too; incidentally, Geoff gets a parcel of shares as *his* reward."

Jenny could have told Drew that her father had lots of horses, that he *bred* them. But she couldn't disappoint him. He really thought he was doing something great for her; it was in the expression on his face. And just then Nat Barrett arrived, in company with Nicole.

He stood behind Drew's shoulder, Nicole hung upon Drew's arm, and they all three looked benignly upon Jenny as if they were giving her a prize of great significance.

"Excuse me, Boss!" the stockman who had first spoken to Jenny was fidgeting with his ten-bale hat. "Excuse me, but that young feller bringing in the horse is coming up the waste paddock in back of the old railway line. If you go over to the wire fence you'll see his dust coming up the rise right now."

They all went out then, and stood on their toes; but only the six-foot-four stockman could see that dust.

Nicole said, "Excuse me, I have things to do. And I fear we're going to have a scene any moment."

She was excused. But she did not go away, after all.

"Come on over to the wire fence, Jenny," Drew called to her.

She supposed she must do that. She certainly didn't want to be ungrateful. But she could almost cry, because that was just exactly what she was. How was she to get the horse to Yaraandoo, for instance? But Geoff was coming. (Oh, thank God for that!) Somehow she wouldn't feel so desperately out of gear with herself when he got here. Suddenly Geoff seemed very dear to her—almost as if she could not do without him. Oh, Geoff!

The stockman led her to the wire fence, and now Jenny, too, could see the dust cloud. Then she could also see the form of a young horse carrying its rider at a gallop.

Only one horse could ever gallop *exactly* like that.

"Beautiful," she said, her voice cracking on the last syllable.

Man and animal in their dust cloud came nearer and nearer.

Oh, Geoff! Jenny was saying in her heart. She was afraid to believe what her eyes were telling her.

It was Geoff, all right. He rode in that funny, heavy, yet commanding way of his—just as she remembered him going round and about on his funny old nag back there in Yaraandoo.

Only this wasn't a funny old nag. This was, this was—It had to be! It *was!*

Tears were in her eyes as she battled her way through the horizontal wires of the old sagging fence. She flew, her hair streaming out behind her, down the paddock towards the horseman coming at a canter now.

Her arms were flung out wide as she ran almost as if she would gather all—man *and* horse—in her arms.

Geoff slowed to a walk,

Then he and his mount came home to Jenny, together.

"Redcoat! Redcoat!" Jenny cried. Then: Geoff! Oh, darling Geoff! I couldn't find you!"

Geoff threw his right leg over the pommel, kicked his other foot free of the stirrup, and slid to the ground. As he came down he threw Redcoat's reins to Jenny. She caught them with her left hand.

"From me to you," Geoff said. "Because I love you, Jenny."

Both his arms went round her as she stood there holding Redcoat's reins, a whole world of love and gratitude in her eyes.

"Redcoat's come home at last," he said. He bent his head and kissed her. Then suddenly he held her tight and kissed her again. And because she kissed him, too, it was quite a long time before he lifted his head or took his arms from around her.

"I think this is where we quietly steal away," Drew said with a smile to Nicole.

"Good luck to them," Nicole agreed. "And it *was* luck that the buyer of that horse was Nat's neighbour. A sheer fluke. She looked at him. "The way she used to speak of that horse, it seemed to be the thing she loved best in the world! It was a stroke of genius to put Geoff in charge of her. *The young inevitably call to the young —in the end.* Don't you agree, darling?"

"Oh, wholeheartedly, my dear!" He glanced over his shoulder at Geoff and Jenny. "Don't turn around now, but the three of them—girl, man, *and* horse—seem at this moment to be welded together."

Nicole put her hand in the crook of Drew's arm. She did *not* turn around.

Only the stockman, a stranger, was interested in what was happening west of where he stood. He looked out into a blaze of glory—red, gold, amethyst, and blue; it was the sun going down.

Guess the next trail for that young pair and their four-footed friend, thought the stockman, was back home to—what was the name of that place down in the country? Oh, yes. *Yaraandoo.* Wasn't that the likes of those down-south people! Come today, gone tomorrow! Ah, well! He could only wish 'em good luck.

The last of the sun was slipping below the horizon. Neither Geoff, Jenny, nor Redcoat seemed to notice it; they were too wrapt in each other.

Blimey! the stockman said to himself. Can't they wait till the flaming sun goes right down?

Geoff had his arms around Jenny and was kissing her again, very meaningfully, too.

"So, that's the way they pass the time in that Yaraandoo,'" reflected the stockman philosophically. "Must go there some day and learn about it myself."

DRAGONMEDE

a novel by
Rona Randall

"There's a new star in the gothic firmament! Rona Randall handles the brooding romantic atmosphere with style and conviction, drawing her readers on enticingly and serving up just what they long for in the way of thrills and chills!"
— *Publishers Weekly*

"Randall has told a fuller and different story better ... about Eustacia ... Julian ... Dragonmede ... and its ancient curse."
— *Kirkus*

"Extremely well told and engrossing ... an interesting and unpredictable tale."
— *Bestsellers*

$1.75